Adam Fitzroy

Between Now and Then

Manifold Press

Published by Manifold Press

ISBN: 978-1-908312-81-5

Proof-reading and line editing: W.S. Pugh

Editor: Fiona Pickles

Text: © Adam Fitzroy 2013
Cover image: © Ann Taylor-Hughes | iStockphoto.com
E-book format: © Manifold Press 2013
Print format: © Julie Bozza 2015
Set in Adobe Garamond Pro

Characters and situations described in this book are fictional and not intended to portray real persons or situations whatsoever; any resemblances to living individuals are entirely coincidental.

For further details of Manifold Press titles both in print and forthcoming: manifoldpress.co.uk

Other titles by Adam Fitzroy:
    The Bridge on the River Wye
    Dear Mister President
    Ghost Station
    Make Do and Mend
    Stage Whispers

Acknowledgements

Thank you to Louise, Morgan and W.S.,
who all helped to make this possible,
and also to 'anon' for double-checking the
Francais.

1

Dennis, who had been drowsing in his seat with his arms folded and his head down, woke up abruptly when the side door of the minibus was violently wrenched open and the icy cold air of a November day hit him with full force.

"Will you shut that bloody thing, you pillock!" he grumbled irritably.

"Now, now," came the maddening response. "*Language, Timothy!*"

If there was one thing that annoyed him about Gary – and there were actually, Dennis reflected, several things – it was the occasional propensity to talk in television catch-phrases as if he'd never had an original thought of his own. In fact, perhaps he hadn't. Not that this seemed to trouble Gary's impressionable younger girlfriend Greta, who was even now emerging like a sleepy snail from the shelter of a fake-fur-lined hood and a multi-coloured Fair Isle scarf. She wore sheepskin mittens, had large brown eyes like a tarsier's, and stared around her as though struggling to remember where she was, who she was with, and perhaps more importantly why on earth she'd bothered to come along at all.

"Is this still Germany?" she asked, shivering.

"Yes, luv," Dennis told her, almost fondly, "it is." Greta was just about the only person on this trip who hadn't got spectacularly up Dennis's nose during the past few days; even Angus – colloquially known as 'Gus the Bus' – with whom in recent years he'd shared the rent of a flat. They were also co-owners of the increasingly clapped-out Toyota Hiace – green with one blue door, after an unfortunate encounter with a Honda on the A64 – in which they were making this voyage of the damned. Gary himself was bidding fair to be dropped overboard from the ferry with extreme prejudice on the way home. "Your boyfriend's been adding to his extensive collection of multi-coloured European bog seats," he added.

To Dennis's amusement, this information actually made Greta sit up and begin to evince a positive interest. "So what was it this time then, Gaz? Orange?"

"No." Gary slammed the sliding door almost in triumph, his fat backside squelching onto the seat he had been occupying throughout the journey. "Purple."

"Bugger off." This comment emerged from somewhere on the seat behind them, where Allan was sprawled out languidly with a blanket over him, his eyes firmly closed, bearing a striking resemblance to Dylan from *The Magic Roundabout*. Indeed, until this moment, nobody had been quite sure whether he was asleep or only pretending, although the absence of snoring seemed to indicate that he had merely chosen to opt out – for which Dennis, although he cordially disliked the man, could scarcely find it in his heart to blame him. After all, they'd been cramped together in a tin can since Sunday afternoon, and this was Thursday; it was an ordeal which would have challenged even the sincerest of friendships, which this most emphatically wasn't. On the other hand, Allan himself wasn't above provoking an argument about things that didn't concern him and which didn't matter anyway, if for some bizarre reason of his own it suited him to do so, and after a while that had become intensely aggravating – as it was becoming yet again in the present case. "Why the hell would anybody want a purple toilet seat?"

"Ain't got a fuckin' clue, mate," responded Gary, blithely, "but that's what it was, purple. And since nobody here had any money on purple, the pot gets carried over into the next round – wherever we end up stopping tomorrow."

"Pot," repeated Allan in a tone of amused disgust, promptly tuning out again completely. "Betting a pot on a pot. Seems oddly appropriate, somehow."

It did indeed, thought Dennis. And this was what they were reduced to – taking bets on the colours of the toilet seats at rest stops along the way. Only in the men's toilets, though, that was the rule; Greta was the sole female on the trip, and her claim to have sat on a pink one somewhere in Holland was therefore ruthlessly discounted – notwithstanding that there had been pale blue in the men's cubicles next door – because there hadn't been a second person available to corroborate the evidence. That was where the game had started, actually, born out of the argument that followed her assertion, and ruefully he supposed it was marginally more imaginative than playing I-Spy. Nonetheless Dennis was bored with discussions about toilet seats – as, in truth, he was thoroughly bored with eating food he didn't understand, with people farting in the minibus, and with conversations which seemed to go round and round and round in ever-decreasing circles. Worse than all this, however, was the leaden sensation that he was ultimately responsible for the entire farrago; it had largely been his idea, with a certain amount of enthusiastic encouragement from Gus, and it had seemed quite reasonable with a few drinks inside him – a bit ambitious, perhaps – but none of it had worked out exactly the way he'd been hoping it would.

In theory it should have been relatively straightforward, if not easy. The Berlin Wall was down at last, and travel to East Germany – or just 'Germany', as the world was again learning to call the reunited halves – was suddenly a practical possibility, as it hadn't been for a generation or more when he was growing up. Add in the fact that England were due to play Poland in Poznań in a qualifying match for the 1992 European Championship Final in Sweden, and also that Dennis and Angus had got through a positively heroic quantity of Newcastle Brown, and they had applied for the tickets before they quite realised what they were letting themselves in for.

Organising the trip had been a total bugger. They'd advertised throughout the hospital, and originally eight people had agreed to go along and share the cost of the journey. Three had dropped out however, lacking – according to Dennis – even half-way decent excuses for doing so. Fortunately they'd all paid non-returnable deposits, which hadn't prevented two of them pleading poverty and attempting to get their money back anyway; their names would be permanently off Dennis's Christmas card list in future. As for the third, he'd negligently allowed himself to be knocked off his motorbike in the middle of October and was languishing in hospital, with steel pins securing both his legs, until just before the day when they'd been due to set off; he at least would have had some excuse for trying to get a refund, but he'd done no such thing. Hadn't even thought of it, in fact. Instead, he'd cursed his rotten luck and benevolently lent Dennis his camera, telling him to take plenty of pictures – which Dennis, an indifferent photographer at the best of times, had promptly subcontracted. It was fortunate – from that point of view, if from no other – that the unexpected last-minute solution to the problem had turned out to be Scarborough Royal Infirmary's new medical photographer, a man none of them had really had a chance to get to know. This, however, was the point at which Dennis ran out of anything positive to say about Allan Ogilvie, except that when this trip was over he hoped he'd never have to set eyes on the miserable sod again as long as the pair of them should live. He was grateful, in fact, not to have had to share a room with him; the non-confrontational Brian, thin-faced and bespectacled, the closest thing to an intellectual in the party, had taken one for the team there – but so far he seemed to have lived to tell the tale.

Gary had not yet finished speaking, however. The sound of the zipper on his leather bomber jacket was loud in the confined space, and so was his demonic cackle as he produced from within – still warm where it had been folded tight against his body – a sheaf of luridly coloured paper.

"Bonus prize," he declaimed in triumph. "Genuine German porn!"

"Oh?" Despite himself, Dennis was more than a little intrigued. "But you don't even speak German." Indeed Gary had given plenty of evidence of this on the trip, and when it came to Polish he had struggled even more. So had they all, in fact; only Angus and Brian seemed to have any fluency in foreign languages, but Brian was a bit of a swot anyway and Gus had seen a hell of a lot of war movies in his time; some of that had been bound to rub off eventually. "You won't be able to read a word of it."

"Ah, well," chortled Gary, offensively pleased with himself, "porn is a universal language! Anyway, there's not a lot of actual reading involved – they're photo stories, and I don't think I'll have too much trouble with them. Look!" He scrubbed through the pages, opening them out apparently at random to a picture of a girl with spectacular mammary development – wearing nothing but a pair of spike-heeled boots, a mask and a pair of studded wristbands – applying a cat-o'-nine-tails to an under-sized man ineffectually shielding his genitals with his hands. Gary was quite right about that; words would have been superfluous, and it wasn't difficult to imagine what either of the parties would be thinking.

"Well, yes," Dennis could hardly help murmuring, "that's clear enough. This is quality stuff, you know; where'd you find it, then?"

"Stuck behind a pipe in the bog. Don't know if anybody was planning to come back and collect it or not, but if they were they've missed their bloody chance; finders keepers, that's what I say!"

"Nice one. You sure the pages aren't all stuck together, though?"

"Not yet they're not," laughed Gary, "but I'm not saying they won't be, by the time I've finished. Hours of harmless entertainment to be got out of this, in my opinion. Or maybe put in to it," he added crudely.

"It isn't hygienic, though, is it?" protested Allan, re-joining the conversation – albeit still with a maddening air of detachment, as if he didn't care and couldn't find a reason to. "Bringing back something you picked up in a public toilet; you have no idea who might've been handling it, for a start. You're all health service workers, for fuck's sake, you really should know better. Why don't you chuck the bloody thing away?"

Dennis, who had considered making a very similar point, immediately reversed his opinion on the subject.

"Oh, leave him alone, you nelly, you're talking like somebody's maiden aunt. Where's the harm in a bit of honest dirty fun, eh, man?"

"'Dirty' is exactly the word for it," responded Allan in disdain. "You know as well as I do, Gary, there could be all sorts of pathogens clinging to those pages. And anyway, you shouldn't be waving that sort of thing about in front of Greta; it's hardly the way to treat a lady, is it?"

"Coo, Gladys, get you!" responded Gary, with a laugh. "Not too many 'ladies' round here, as far as I can see – or 'gentlemen' either, unless you reckon you're one." A disgusted snort expressed his opinion of this idea. "And you should see some of the things I wave about in front of her when we're at home, anyway. She doesn't seem to mind about that too much – do you, eh, Greet?"

"Oh well," returned Allan in a tone of icy sarcasm, "in that case, I take it all back. Clearly you're a model of deportment, and your life together must be utterly enchanting. Greta's a very lucky girl."

"Just what I keep telling her," said Gary, on whom the sarcasm was entirely wasted. "But she doesn't appreciate me."

Greta was casting a jaded eye in the direction of the magazine. "I've seen worse," she admitted. "I like that leopard-print rug, though – and the mirror in the background; I wonder where she bought it?" And that, it seemed, was as much as she was prepared to say for now, although she continued looking over Gary's shoulder as he flickered industriously through the pages.

"Thus setting the cause of Women's Liberation back another decade or two," mumbled Allan, subsiding into his seat.

"Yeah, as if you really cared about that," scoffed Dennis, returning to the fray.

"You have no idea, Dennis, whether I care about it or not," returned Allan, in a massively dispirited tone. "You don't have the first clue about me, and what I might or might not happen to believe in. For all you know I might be at the forefront of the feminist movement."

"You're not, though, are you?" Dennis challenged.

"As it happens, I'm not, but that isn't the point. The point is that you're making unwarranted assumptions about me, without any evidence to back them up."

"Is that so? Well, I might as well make a couple more, then, in that case. For example, I could start by assuming that you're a wanker who could whinge for England – and there's plenty of evidence to back that one up. Actually, now that I come to think about it, that may be everything about you that I'll ever really need to know."

"Well, speaking for myself," put in Greta, "there's nothing I need liberating from, anyway; most of the men I know couldn't oppress their way out of a paper bag – not without a woman to help them."

"I know," returned Allan. "But that's precisely what the patriarchal hegemony wants you to think, isn't it? You've had one woman Prime Minister and now you think everything in the garden's going to be lovely? Honestly, you're deluded! 'Once you familiarise yourself with the chains of bondage you prepare your own limbs to wear them', that's what Abraham Lincoln said." He turned away after this as if, having delivered what he clearly expected to be a fatal blow to the argument, he could no longer bear to look upon the carnage.

"'Chains of bondage'?" Gary laughed a vulgar little laugh. "I never knew Lincoln was into all that kinky stuff. He'd've enjoyed this lot, then." And he returned to enthusiastic appreciation of the magazine, whilst a sullen silence fell over the other inhabitants of the van.

Dennis, left to contemplate the bizarre way the conversation had spiralled out of control – from toilet seats to Thatcherism to the politics of oppression – watched the pink-neon-bordered doorway of the rest area's convenience store like a cat watches a mouse hole, until at long last the door swung open and the missing members of their party, Angus and Brian, came striding down the steps clutching their purchases.

"Thank fuck for that," he murmured. "Here come the bloody cavalry at last." And immediately wished he hadn't, when Gary's toneless impersonation of a cavalry bugle bounced loudly around inside the minibus. Allan's despairing groan in response, however, was almost worth the pain.

Gus carried a plastic bag in each hand and Brian's arms were full of packaged bottles, as a result of which he struggled to open the sliding door. When he had, though, he pushed his bounty in and climbed after it with the self-satisfied air of a caveman dragging home a slaughtered deer for lunch. "Success!" he proclaimed delightedly.

"Everything?" Greta was immediately awake again, and even Allan's torpor seemed temporarily dispelled as he sat up and took notice of events.

"Everything. Allan's wine and brandy, Pernod for Gaz's mum, Calvados for me, and enough German beer to get us most of the way home. I'll shove it on the back seat for now and we can settle up when we get to the hotel, all right? I can't wrap my brain around it at the moment."

"Took you long enough," observed Allan. "Busy in there, was it?"

"As a matter of fact, it was." Angus handed in his own packages before walking around to the driver's door and taking his seat again, pushing the keys into the ignition with the casual arrogance of ownership. "They've got some kind of bloody special offer on so the place is heaving, and we got a wee bit side-tracked by the TV; there was something on the news about Turdo Ferries." It had been predestined from the moment they had made the booking; Turbo Ferries were by far the cheapest carrier providing ferry services out of Hull, and in actual fact the accommodation on the way over had been perfectly acceptable, but a name like that guaranteed that they would always be known – by this group of travellers at least – as something different. It was just too good a pun to miss.

"Well?" demanded Dennis, "what was it?"

"Don't know – they didn't have the sound on, just the picture. We waited to see if came round again before we paid for our stuff but it didn't, so we'll have to wait to get back to the hotel before we can find out what it was." Gus twisted the keys, and the engine woke from slumber. "Everybody ready?" Brian, who had clambered through to sit beside him and was fastening his seatbelt, nodded assent. Nobody else did more than groan in weary acknowledgement, which Angus took little notice of anyway. "All right then, let's get this show on the road."

A quick check of the rear-view mirror, a judicious application of the clutch, and the minibus began to roll forward. And not before time, either, thought Dennis; personally he couldn't wait to get home and put all these people back into their proper boxes in his mind. That was precisely where he wanted to be able to keep them all, too, after this was all over – with the notable exception of Angus – at arm's length and completely out of his hair, and for the rest of his bloody life if there was any justice in the world.

2

The hotel in Berlin was one of those old-fashioned independent ones with wrought-iron balconies – there was a scandalised murmur from Gary that 'the enemy' still had all their wrought-iron whilst we had sacrificed ours for Spitfires during the war – and a green canopy over the door; the bathrooms were communal and spaced out along the corridors, and all the furniture was twenty years out of date. Nevertheless it was cheap, conveniently located for everything they were ever likely to need, and homely and comfortable compared to the soulless concrete edifice they'd occupied in Poznań. Just as it had been last night and the night before, theirs was a weary routine – park the minibus, take out the luggage, check in, then separate into their component parts – Allan and Brian to one room, Gary and Greta to a second, Dennis and Angus trudging towards a third. This time, however, their room looked out onto a pleasant small courtyard – not much more than a light well – which housed one tree and a few neglected flower beds. It was a nice room, too, clean and fresh and quiet; it was just a shame to waste it on two unappreciative louts such as themselves who only cared about showering, sleeping, washing their socks and raiding the minibar – and not necessarily in that order.

Arrangements for their evening meal had been purposely left vague. There was a McDonalds on the corner, a Pizza Hut in the middle of the next block, and room service of a sort provided you were willing pay twice the price for your food to be microwaved by the hall porter. Dennis, having armed himself with a phrasebook which would allow him to translate a fast food menu, was all for venturing into the city as soon as they'd scattered their belongings and claimed their beds. Angus, however, had opened the windows and was leaning on the rail of the shallow Juliet balcony, looking down into the courtyard below.

"I think," he said slowly, his soft Scots accent always more pronounced when he was tired, "we need to find out what's the matter with Turdo Ferries first. I didn't want to say anything in front of the others, but if there's something up we're going to need all the information we can get our hands on before we leave here in the morning."

"What d'you mean, 'something up'?" Resigned to the fact that they were not going to be eating immediately, Dennis levered his shoes off and wiggled his toes to bring his feet back to life a bit; sitting still for long periods didn't really suit him, nor did being a passenger when someone else was driving – even if that someone did happen to be Angus.

"They had a headline running across the screen," supplied Gus. "Something about *Unglücksfall.* That means some kind of accident, but it could be anything from a breakdown to a major disaster. We might just have a bit of difficulty getting home."

"What d'you mean difficulty? You mean they've sunk the bloody thing?" It was less than five years since the sinking of the *Herald of Free Enterprise* had seared its name into the British national consciousness; surely there couldn't have been another ferry lost in the same waters quite so soon? He'd made sure for himself that the vessel they'd been on hadn't left port with its bow doors open; in fact he'd been one of a group of passengers standing up there on the highest deck, listening as the wretched things clanged into place and the bolts shot home, braving the scornful glances of the crew. But every traveller knew, now, that a commonplace journey like this one had the potential to be dangerous, and everybody wanted to make sure it never happened again. Dennis wasn't the only person, he knew, following the slow progress of construction on the Channel Tunnel with more than ordinary interest.

"I don't think so, but it could have broken down or run aground or something, or maybe they've just hit the harbour wall with it." To a generation raised on the comedy antics of *HMS Troutbridge,* this did not seem too unlikely. "Or it could be a strike, maybe; anything's possible. We'll get the English news in half an hour," Gus added, gesturing towards the TV in the corner of the room. "I don't want to do anything about food until after that, just in case we have to come up with a Plan B. You go on, though, if you want to."

Which was typical of Angus, really, now that Dennis thought about it. He might act the fool from time to time, especially when he'd been on the juice, but give him a measure of responsibility for the lives and well-being of other people and he rose to the challenge magnificently. Angus was always thinking ahead; that was one of his finer – and also his more annoying – qualities.

"No," said Dennis. "I'll wait. I wouldn't mind grabbing a shower, if I can find a bathroom free."

"Good. I'll have a smoke and a coffee, then, and see if I can find the right channel on the telly."

"Sounds like a fair division of labour to me." Dennis dug out clean underwear, and gathered up a hotel towel and the free shampoo. "Wish me luck on my travels."

"Oh aye," said Gus obligingly, "good luck," as the room door closed between them and Dennis set off in search of the facilities.

Half an hour later, having done battle with an unusually perverse shower unit, Dennis returned to find Angus in a somewhat bloody frame of mind. He had been about to ask whether there was news, but the expression on his room-mate's face was prohibitively discouraging.

"They've gone bust," he declared, abruptly. "Turns out Turdo Ferries were deep in the shite long before they ever took our booking. They owe the Inland Revenue more than half a million quid, which is why they've put in a winding-up petition and impounded all their bloody boats – which means we're probably not going to get a ferry back the way we came over. There's a phone number to check for places, but I've already tried it a couple of times and it's permanently engaged. Anyway, BBC reckon other ferry companies have agreed to take up the slack, but there's no hope of anything out of Rotterdam for at least a couple of days – not with a vehicle, anyway; they're still taking foot passengers. So we'd either have to leave the bus behind or fork out for a couple of nights in a hotel somewhere while we wait. Alternatively they say we can make for one of the channel ports – Calais or Boulogne or somewhere – where they're going to have more sailings; they're apparently honouring Turdo tickets on a first-come first-served basis."

"Calais?" Dennis fixed on the word and repeated it in bewilderment.

"How far away's that, then?"

Angus shrugged. "I didn't bring my big European road atlas," he said. "I didn't think we'd need it, so we'll have to go out and buy a map. I reckon it's maybe … five, six hundred miles. Actually not a lot further than Rotterdam, but we'll have to go all the way through Belgium first."

"Plus we'll be landing at the wrong end of the country and we'll have to get back to Yorkshire from there, so what's that – another three hundred miles on top?"

"About that, depending on where we end up, but I don't think we've got much choice – and with any luck, we could be home by tea-time on Saturday, just in time to get the football results."

Dennis ran a thoughtful hand across his stubbled chin. "The others know anything about this yet?"

"Obviously not, or they'd have been in here breaking my balls about it," returned Angus cynically. "Brian was going to have a bath, Allan's probably asleep, and I dread to think what Gary and Greta are up to; trying out some of the stuff in that porno mag, I wouldn't be surprised." He shuddered, as though the images this notion conjured up were just too hideous to contemplate.

"So we'd better have a solution ready for them before they realise there's even a problem, hadn't we?"

"Aye, that's exactly what I was thinking. How about you stay here and keep trying that phone number, while I go out and see if I can get us a map?"

Sighing, Dennis draped his towel over the back of the chair and reached out to switch on the kettle. The day was getting longer and longer, and steadily worse and worse, and he'd had more than enough of it a very long time ago.

"All right," he conceded. "You know, this might all have been worth it if only it had been a decent match – but what with getting roughed up by the cops in Poznań and then that twat Mabbutt getting in the way of a free kick it's been more or less a fuckin' disaster all round. And that's not even counting bloody Allan."

Angus, an unrepentant old hippie with long pepper-and-salt hair, was climbing into an RAF surplus greatcoat with a bizarre assortment of cloth badges sewn onto the sleeves; NO NUKES, SAVE THE WHALE, LED ZEPPELIN. He wound a Doctor Who scarf around his neck; it was close to full dark outside already, and the threat of snow was hanging in the air.

"I don't know what you've got against the poor sod," he said, "but I don't find him all that offensive; he's quiet enough, he doesn't bother anybody."

"He bothers me," protested Dennis. "He's like nails on a blackboard, he sets my teeth on edge. I feel like nothing anybody does will ever be good enough for him. I feel like he's looking down his nose at all of us – and at me in particular."

"Well, if he is," said Angus, "I can't say I've noticed anything myself. You don't suppose that could just be paranoia on your part?"

"It could," conceded Dennis magnanimously. "But just because you're paranoid, it doesn't mean they're not all out to get you. I don't trust that bastard as far as I can throw him, that's all – and at the moment, that wouldn't be very far."

By the time Gus was back from his shopping trip – Dennis was impressed that he'd managed to locate the map he wanted and buy it in a foreign language in so short a time – there was still no reply from the number the BBC had been giving out, and the demands of food were therefore allowed to take precedence. Rounding up the others, therefore, they made their way out to the nearest Pizza Hut, where they pushed two tables together and got on surprisingly quickly with the complicated business of ordering. Then – after the first beers had arrived, and while they were waiting for their food – Gus produced the map and outlined the problem they were facing.

"As far as I can see," he said, "our best bet would be to go back more or less the way we came, then turn south towards Antwerp – but not until we're far enough west. There's a couple of roads we could take." His fingers skated across the surface of the map. "Either way, it's going to be at least eight hours' solid driving, not counting stops, so it's a good job there's two of us." He glanced at Dennis, receiving only a resigned shrug by way of answer.

The others, looking at the map, seemed to be struggling to take it all in.

"How are we going to manage about money?" asked Allan, eventually. "We only brought Deutschmarks and a few zlotys."

"True. We can try changing some of our marks in the morning before we set off, though, and if everything else fails there's always plastic."

"What is it they have in Belgium, anyway? Francs?"

"Yes. Well, that and bloody Euros, but I'm not having anything to do with them if I can help it. What I reckon we should probably do is head for Zeebrugge in the first instance, and see if we can get home from there. If not, we've got Ostend, Dunkirk, Calais, Boulogne, Dieppe … we'll just have to keep going until we can find a space on something."

"Oh god, it'll be just like that bloody film … what was it, *The Cassandra Crossing*?" Gary was trying to pick the design off the outside of his beer glass with a thumbnail, and failing. "We'll end up trundling over a cliff somewhere and falling into the sea."

"No bad thing if it actually means you getting a bath, mate," observed Brian, waspishly.

"Yeah, funny man," returned Gary. "You know, one day they'll get that bloody Chunnel finished and we'll just be able to drive on through it and be home in half an hour."

"I'm not sure it'll be quite as easy as all that," Angus put in, mildly, "but I'd be very grateful for a nice reliable tunnel just at the moment, rather than having to dick about looking for a ferry company willing to very kindly honour tickets that we've paid good money for."

"Would you really fancy that, though, Gus?" Dennis asked him. "All that bloody water up above your head? Supposing it broke in on you, and you drowned?"

"Wouldn't be a lot I could do about it if it happened, would there?" Angus pointed out reasonably. "Once you're down there you're down there and there's no way out."

"Just what I'm saying," returned Dennis. "At least if the boat sinks you've got a bit of a chance."

"Not much of one, though," said Brian, reaching down from some Olympian height to touch the conversation for a moment. "And drowning's a nasty way to go. I know some bloody good people who drowned; I wouldn't wish that on anybody, really."

"Oh? Anybody in particular?"

"Well, there was Shelley."

"Shelley who? Oh, that girl who used to work in the canteen? Yeah, I remember her; never knew she was dead, though."

"No, Gary, not the girl in the canteen, Shelley the poet. Percy Bysshe – that Shelley."

"Oh, him. Poof, wasn't he?"

"You are a pig ignorant son of a bitch, Gareth," said Brian, without malice. "And whether he was a poof or not is beside the point. Listen to this:

Peace, peace! he is not dead, he doth not sleep
He hath awakened from the dream of life
'Tis we, who lost in stormy visions, keep
With phantoms an unprofitable strife,
And in mad trance, strike with our spirit's knife
Invulnerable nothings."

"I've heard that somewhere before," said Dennis, puzzled. "What's it from?"

"*Adonais.* Mick Jagger read it out on the stage in Hyde Park after Brian Jones died."

"Oh yeah, I remember. Seen that on the telly."

"Well, I was there," said Brian, unexpectedly. "I was seventeen. It was the first time I'd ever been to London and it scared the pants off me, if you really want to know, but I totally loved that bit. What a great way to be remembered!"

"Aye, it was," concurred Angus. "I always thought so. I wouldn't mind somebody remembering me like that, when the time comes."

"You actually think any of us'll ever be remembered?" asked Dennis sourly. "It's not like we're famous or anything, is it? We're just a bloody bunch of plonkers from Yorkshire."

"Speak for yourself," laughed Brian. "I'm not a plonker! My granddad used to say nobody ever really dies as long as there's someone alive who still remembers them – and he was in the trenches in the First

World War, so he ought to know. Anyway I'll make you a deal – I'll remember you, you remember me, and we'll both remember Gus and Allan and Greta."

"Here, what about me?" protested Gary.

"In your case, mate, I reckon forgetting you would be the problem!"

"Cheeky sod. But you're right, though – I am pretty unique."

"Unique maybe," amended Allan. "Not exactly pretty, though."

"Well, that's a matter of opinion, sunshine."

"Wait a minute." Greta, as usual, stepped in before the banter could get out of hand and subtly diverted them to another topic. "Wasn't that the gig where Jagger wore a frilly dress?"

"It was supposed to be a Greek soldier's tunic," commented Brian rationally, "but yes, that's right."

"And the reason for that," opined Gary, "is that he's a poof too. Did you see him all over Bowie on *Live Aid*? As queer as an ice-skater's friend!"

"So what?" challenged Allan. "Is it anybody's business but their own?"

"Well, yeah, I happen to think it is. They shouldn't be doing it in bloody public and expecting people to pay to see it, should they? It's immoral, that is!" Which, thought Dennis, was a bit of double standard coming from a man who clearly had no qualms about enjoying pornography.

"Nice work if you can get it, though," Brian told him, his mouth curving into a mischievous smile, and mercifully for the sanity of everyone concerned that was precisely the point at which their massive order of pizzas and garlic bread had providentially chosen to arrive.

3

No-one was very keen to get started the following morning. Dennis, having been 'volunteered' for the first stint of driving, took his time going over the maps with Angus as soon as they were sufficiently awake, and together they formed what might almost have been said to resemble a plan.

"The tricky bit's getting out of Berlin," he sighed. "Once we're on the right road we keep going as far as Duisburg, and shortly after that we pick up this one which takes us into Holland at Venlo. After that we head towards Antwerp and Ghent, and the next bit depends on which ferry port we're going to."

"Which depends on whether or not we can get through to this so-called emergency number," responded Gus, without enthusiasm. He'd spent some considerable time already this morning clinging to an unresponsive receiver whilst the 'engaged' signal rang in his ear, and he was doing it again now. "Bastards couldn't organise the proverbial in a brewery," he opined. "English, I bet; can't start work in the morning until they've had a cup of tea."

"Well, what d'you have in Scotland, haggis juice?" Dennis sipped his own tea by way of rejoinder, but it had been poor stuff to start with and long-life milk had only made it worse. They didn't understand tea in Germany, he'd decided. "Whisky?"

"The only good reason to have whisky at breakfast time is still being pissed from the night before," Angus informed him flatly. "Look, Den, we'll have to assume these buggers aren't going to be much help and set off anyway. We can call again whenever we stop." Resignedly, he put the phone down. "You okay with Allan navigating for you on the first bit?"

"I suppose so; it's not as if there's much choice, is it?"

"No, it's not," conceded Gus. "Hopefully most of it's straight-forward, but you'll need somebody to guide you out of Berlin – and I wouldn't want to rely on Gary if I didn't have to; that wee loon's got the attention span of a goldfish."

"True enough. If it isn't wearing football boots or a peep-hole bra, he doesn't want to know. No, I'd rather have Allan – which is saying something. As long as I don't have to talk to him too much, and I don't actually have to listen to him at all!"

"Well, stick some bloody music on and listen to that instead." Angus's bushy eyebrows waggled wickedly.

"Oh, yeah, right." And that had been a bone of contention too, of course. Everybody has brought such a varied selection of cassettes with them that by the time the first round of arguments was over Chris Rea's 'Road to Hell' had been just about the only thing they all agreed on. By the fourth or fifth iteration of that, however, they'd been just as happy to settle for the patchy reception and incomprehensible speech of various Continental music stations, or to switch off altogether and sit in what passed – at the best of times – for companionable silence. Conversation had always been tricky; what with the list of banned topics getting longer and longer, coloured toilet seats would very soon be the only subject they had left that it would be remotely safe to talk about.

When Gus and Dennis reached the dining room, Allan and Brian were there already; they had a German newspaper open on the table, from which Brian was translating a fierce debate about whether Borussia or Eintracht would top the Bundesliga this season, whilst Allan dug morosely through a bowl of fruit salad.

"Anything about the ferries?" asked Dennis, although he could guess already that there wouldn't be. The collapse of a small German ferry company would hardly make the headlines in England, and it wasn't reasonable to expect the reverse to be true. Still, there might have been a line or two.

"Nothing," said Brian, "it's all German news. On the bright side, I did manage to get some Belgian francs – fifty quid's worth – for incidentals along the way. Had to put it on my credit card, though."

"Well, at least you've got a credit card," murmured Dennis. Living more or less hand-to-mouth as he did, such things were scarcely even on his radar. "So we'll be able to get something to eat in Belgium, and petrol if we need it."

"We should be all right for petrol," Gus predicted thoughtfully. "If we fill up this morning as soon as we're out of the city, and again just before we leave Germany. I reckon we can get across Belgium on about half a tank, so we shouldn't have to buy any more after that until we're back in England. Anyway, as long as we're on motorways and major roads there should be plenty of chances."

"We're all set then, are we?" asked Brian. "No luck with the phone, I suppose?"

"Not a chance. And yes, I think we're ready – all packed, anyway; just the bill to settle before we leave."

"But what about Love's Young Dream?" put in Allan. "Anybody seen them so far this morning?"

"No. You know what they're like; they won't be out of bed yet, and then Greta'll have to wash her hair, and then they'll have to have breakfast. I can't see us getting on the road much before ten o'clock."

"Which is bloody inconsiderate of them, to say the least," returned Allan, sourly. "The rest of us are up and ready to go; I don't see why we have to stand around waiting while the pair of them get their act together."

"Well, they can't exactly get home without us," Brian pointed out emolliently.

"All the more reason for them to be on time, I'd've thought."

"Well, that's true," re-joined Gus, "but what you're forgetting, Allan, is that the four of us miserable single blokes don't have anything like the excuse Gary does for staying in bed in the mornings – so let's cut the wee bugger a bit of slack, shall we?"

Allan's sniff of disapproval would have been eloquent in just about any language. "Him," he said, "I can understand, if it comes to that, but Greta's a sensible girl; why hasn't she realised that she's far too good for him?"

"I have absolutely no idea," conceded Brian, "but I've seen a lot of women over the years wasting themselves on useless men. I suppose we all get desperate from time to time; don't tell me you've never been desperate, Allan?"

"Not really. Well, not for sex. Until a few months ago I was married," continued Allan, to a response of poorly-camouflaged disbelief. "You're not likely to be all that desperate for it if you're married, are you?"

"You shouldn't be," acknowledged Brian, "but that isn't always true, of course." And that, together with a general unwillingness to ask any further questions about Allan's previously unsuspected marital status, brought this phase of the discussion emphatically to an end.

Gary and Greta emerged from their room around an hour later, just in time to get breakfast before the facilities were withdrawn, and even then they stolidly refused to be rushed. They took their time over eating – deliberately, it seemed to Dennis – then announced that they were going back to their room to pack. The idea that they were so far behind everyone else and had still done nothing about packing was more than a little aggravating, but the others – who had not only settled their bills but also stowed their baggage in the minibus – sat down in the hotel lobby to drink more coffee and wait, in various stages of irascibility, until the couple put in an appearance.

"No point in setting off too early," Gary opined off-handedly, as they settled themselves into the minibus at last. "Get the rush hour out of the way, then we haven't got to deal with the traffic." Which would have been a reasonable enough approach, if only they'd all agreed on it beforehand.

Dennis, resisting the temptation to point out that Gary didn't have to deal with anything – except being on time, and he hadn't even managed that – strapped on his seat-belt and adjusted the rear-view mirror. At his side, Allan had the new road map out as well as the street plan of Berlin; he looked prepared for any eventuality, although his navigational abilities had yet to be put to the test.

"Turn right as you leave the car park, then go straight ahead at the lights," he began crisply, and Dennis grunted acknowledgement. This was going to be interesting – and maybe a little bit too interesting for his peace of mind, like the old Chinese curse. It was not without misgivings that he started up the engine, put the van into gear, and nosed it out through the archway and into the street.

Once they had filled up with petrol and made it out of the city and onto the A2, which for the next several hundred miles was to be their constant companion, the morning disintegrated into a hard and uninspiring slog enlivened only by the discovery of a country and western radio station with its commentary in English. None of them were exactly country and western fans, and in less dire circumstances they might have made suitably scathing remarks about the music, but now it felt like the least worst option available, and at various points over the next couple of hours they all found themselves unconsciously singing along. It was only when Dennis – to his great embarrassment – discovered that he had been joining Don Williams in recalling a gypsy woman, that he realised his attention had begun to wander ever so slightly and that maybe a break was indicated; two hours from Berlin, therefore, he pulled the bus into the parking area of a *Raststätte* and decreed a pause for refreshments. He might just as well have given the order to scatter, given the speed with which the party dispersed in all directions almost before the wheels had stopped moving, and Dennis himself only delayed long enough to lock the bus before he too headed off in the general direction of the food.

They were back on the road half an hour later, labouring through a mixture of rural and industrial scenery, past factories and slurry tanks, deep woodlands and slab-sided warehouses. After a couple of hours of this, as both the sun – already elusive in a sky the colour of ice – and the needle on the fuel gauge began to decline, and conversation in the van dwindled almost to nothing, Dennis felt as if someone was attacking his eyeballs with heavy grit sandpaper. He cranked down his window, allowing cold air and the pitiless whine of the concrete road surface into the driving position, and desperately sought around for some subject he could discuss with his taciturn navigator just to keep himself awake.

"I didn't realise you'd ever been married," he said at last. It wasn't the most tactful opening, now that he came to think about it, but if he didn't find something to take his mind off the monotony of the road he wouldn't be answerable for the consequences.

"Well ... " It was the sort of response that isn't really a response at all. "Like I said, we're divorced. That's why I moved to Scarborough – so I wouldn't keep running into her. She stayed behind in York."

Dennis was silent for a moment, trying to summon up something to say when his brain was a total blank. "Nasty, was it?" he managed, after a struggle.

"It wasn't great. Nobody likes having their private life dragged through the courts, you know."

"No, I don't suppose they do. She divorced you, then, did she?"

"She did. And before you ask – she got the house, the car and the dog and I still have to pay her two hundred quid a month."

"Ouch! Children?"

"None at all, thank fuck; they'd probably have ended up like her, anyway, so that's a relief."

"Sounds as if you've had a bastard of a time," said Dennis. Despite himself, he couldn't help feeling a measure of sympathy; annoyance or not, it was difficult to imagine Allan deserving rough treatment at the hands of his ex, and that sort of thing actually went a long way towards accounting for his diffident and less than cheerful disposition. Women, in Dennis's experience, almost always got the best of it when it came to divorce settlements – which was probably because most of the judges who dealt with them were male.

"Yeah, I did."

"Does she work?"

"She's a radiographer." Allan shifted in his seat. "Look, do we have to talk about this? It's not as if I'd been interrogating you about your private life, is it?"

"No, all right, if that's the way you feel. Just taking an interest, that's all." And really Dennis hadn't cared about the answers he was getting, just about having someone to talk to who'd take the edge off the boredom a bit – even if that someone did have to be Allan. "So, who d'you support, then – York City?"

"Not really, but I've been there a few times; the ground's not far from where we used to live. How about you – Scarborough?"

"Newcastle. That's where my dad came from. He was a big fan all his life."

"Oh, so you inherited it, then, did you?"

"I suppose so. That's the way it works up north – dads, granddads, great-granddads, all supporting the same team. Old-fashioned."

"Traditional," Allan corrected, mildly. "Must be nice to have roots, though. We never really settled anywhere long enough, when I was growing up. My dad was in the Army, so we lived all over the place – Hong Kong, Cyprus, whatever."

"Not Germany, though?"

"No, or I'd probably speak a bit of the language. Well, my dad was here, but only for about eight months; we came to visit over Christmas, but that's the only time I've ever been before – more than thirty years ago. Mum and I stayed with my gran while he was away, and when he got back we all moved up to Catterick. We were still there when he left the Army in 1966, so that's where we stayed. Which is how I ended up in Yorkshire," he added ruefully, "when I was born in Hong Kong."

"Fuck," said Dennis. "I've only ever been on a package holiday to Malaga and a couple of booze cruises to Dieppe. Nothing exotic like that."

"And to a football match in Poland," Allan reminded him. "That was pretty exotic, wasn't it?"

"A bit too bloody exotic, if you ask me; people expect English fans to be violent even when we're not, so they think they have to treat us all like a pack of wild animals – and you get sick of being herded after a while. Did you see that bloke in front of us getting thumped by the riot cop when we first got to the ground? Bashed him right across the back of his legs for no bloody reason, when all the poor bugger was doing was lighting a ciggie."

"Yeah, well, he probably did it in a violent and threatening manner or something," suggested Allan, sniffing sarcastically.

"Probably. Even so, it was a bit of an extreme reaction."

"Very true. What can you expect, though, eh? Foreigners."

And that, thought Dennis, was probably the first time the two of them had ever agreed about anything. They hadn't hit it off, from the moment they'd met, because Allan wasn't exactly outgoing and he always seemed to have a bad smell under his nose. He kept people at a distance wherever he could, only interacting with them on a superficial level; he didn't talk about himself, and didn't encourage anybody else to do so either. With Allan it was the weather, football, work, maybe music, and that was it. Not that music was something they'd ever see eye to eye about, either, what with Allan liking The Housemartins and Dennis preferring The Stones. On the other hand, even The Housemartins had to be better than yet another repeat of bloody Chris Rea – or the eternal steel-guitar twanging of various Chads and Louellas – and maybe there was somewhere in the middle that they could meet without doing one another any actual physical violence.

"What do you think of Gerry Rafferty?" asked Dennis, as if he couldn't have cared less about the answer.

"Don't mind him." Allan's tone was a match for his dismissive words, but nonetheless it was clear that an olive branch of sorts – the merest twig of one, at least – had been extended by one, and grudgingly accepted by the other.

"All right, then. There's a tape of his in the box – put that on. Maybe it'll keep the pair of us awake until we get to the next lot of services at Bottrop."

And Allan, without vouchsafing any further comment, was content to do precisely this, and conversation between them was discontinued for a while.

4

The next break was longer. They stopped to empty their bladders – the seats, disappointingly, were all white – to try the emergency number again, with the usual amount of success, and to eat a meal of mass-produced burgers with chips so thin and dry that they would have done better to eat drinking straws. This they washed down with coffee and soft drinks, before hitting the shop to stock up again on whatever sugar-rich snack foods they could recognise. When at last they returned to the van, Dennis crept gratefully into the back and immediately parked himself with his head leaning on the pane of the side window, whilst Allan stretched out on the seat behind him with his feet resting on Greta's suitcase, wrapped himself in his blanket and made it abundantly clear he would be taking no further part in the proceedings whatsoever.

Not that there was much to take part in, really; another hour in the steadily encroaching twilight brought them at dusk to the border between Germany and Holland at Venlo, an undramatic composition of police station, lorry park, and signage, where the only real indication that they had left one country and entered another was an alteration to the road number and a difference in the language on the direction markers. Neither had much impact on the travellers, since they had only to proceed in a more or less straight line, letting the road do the work for them, until they had crossed into Belgium and reached the outskirts of Antwerp, when they would have to pick up a route south-westwards.

"We'll need to stop somewhere in the region of Ghent," said Brian, turning in the front seat. This was clearly the result of a low, mumbled conversation he'd been having with Angus for some minutes past, barely a word of which had leaked back to the other passengers. "We can stretch our legs, and I'll try the phone again. We've got to know at some point which ferry port it is we're making for."

There was a general murmur of assent, although it would have been fair to suggest that nobody cared enough to have an opinion. If their original plans had come to fruition they would all have been back at Rotterdam by now, safely aboard the Turdo Ferry, and – according to their preference – either tucked up in matchboxy little cabins or leaning on the padded bar wrapping their laughing-gear around pints of Danish lager. Turdo had undoubtedly been cheap and cheerful, but they'd actually had quite a lot going for them – right up until the moment when they'd gone belly-up and left a lot of people scouring their way home across Europe in a gathering gloom that was anything but metaphorical.

Indeed, it was full dark before they stopped at another service station, stumbling wearily towards a brightly-lit interior, going through the routine of relieving themselves, buying refreshments, and staring out of the window towards the headlights rumbling by on the road; low, fast cars full of commuters; large, heavy trucks laden with goods; motorbikes, their hardy riders head down and focussing on the kilometres ahead. It was exhausting just to watch them, and the sounds of the road had penetrated deeply into their nervous systems, effectively scrambling their brains; they had little to say for themselves at this particular stop.

Brian had marched off towards the bank of phones in the lobby with a fatalistic expression on his face, and now came back towards them in the cafeteria clutching a grubby piece of paper and carrying himself with a kind of triumphant jauntiness which had been absent from all of them for most of the day. Seeing his approach, Dennis kicked a chair out for him to sit on.

"Get anywhere this time?" he asked, striving to sound interested.

"Believe it or not, I did. I've got us a booking from Dunkirk – and a confirmation number to go with it. Apparently what you do is show up at the port and give them this number, pay them a fiver a head, and they put you on the next available ferry."

"A fiver each?" approved Gus. "That's not too bad."

"It is when you consider we paid the other buggers ninety quid for the return half of the journey," put in Gary, obstreperously. "Shelling out another thirty on top of that is daylight bloody robbery."

"True – although they don't actually have to take us at all," Brian pointed out, calm in the face of ingratitude. "You want to get home, don't you? Only it'd cost more than that to stay here – and if you don't show up for work the Health Authority just might stop paying you."

"How will they ever know if he's there or not?" asked Angus, chuckling around the rim of his coffee cup. "That wee bugger never does a stroke anyway. I've seen you," he added, "in that store of yours, walking round with a clipboard pretending to be working. Management're gonna get wise eventually, you know."

"Oy, you … " And it could have erupted into a full-scale argument right there and then, under the glaring yellow lights of a Belgian motorway café, had Greta not emerged from her self-imposed cocoon of silence to ask a particularly pertinent question.

"When?" she said to Brian. "I mean, what time?"

Although clearly grateful for the interruption, he grimaced before answering. "Yeah, that's the other thing. They don't want us showing up before eleven o'clock tomorrow; they reckon there's so much demand that they're having to give people timed slots, and even then we might have to wait. Basically there's no point arriving there too early, so we're going to have to find somewhere to stay the night."

"Oh, fuck," groaned Gary. "More bloody expense."

"There's no way round it, I'm afraid – and it's the same for everybody, if that's any consolation."

"It's not," continued Gary, truculently. "I don't want to end up paying for a hotel, Greta and me're short of money as it is. I'd rather sleep in the bloody van."

"Not in November you wouldn't," corrected Gus. "Believe me, I've tried it; everything gets iced up – and we haven't got sleeping bags or anything, just two blankets between the six of us."

"Well, what are you thinking, then?" Plainly Gary was getting close to the end of his tether.

"Keep your hair on; you do realise none of this is my fault, don't you?" Which, in the circumstances, was a milder reproof than the situation merited, and went some way towards calming Gary's agitated nerves. "As a matter of fact, I have got an idea." Gus unfolded the map. "I've been through this area once before, years ago. There's dozens of wee villages scattered about, and they all have places to stay in them; they get a lot of visitors in the summer. There's loads of time, we're only a couple of hours from Dunkirk, so what I suggest we do is head across this way – maybe on this road, or this one – " his fingers traced roughly diagonal lines, "and see what we come up with. There's a couple of small towns we have to pass through; they're bound to have something or other."

He sounded so confident that it took Dennis a moment or two to recognise the flaw in the plan – that they would be looking for accommodation after dark in a place they didn't know, where they had little of the local currency and hardly any familiarity with the language. Nevertheless the traditional resort of the English traveller abroad – speaking his own language loudly and clearly – had got them to Poland and back already; surely, between that and whatever smatterings of French they remembered from school, they should be able to make their requirements understood.

"Well," Allan made his first substantive contribution to the conversation since asking Greta to pass him the sugar, "I wouldn't mind getting off the motorway; I've been sick of the bloody sight of it for hours."

"Right, then, that's settled. We'll leave the motorway at this junction here and head slightly south of west – this road, I think – and if anybody's short of money for their room either Brian or I will spot them for it until we get home."

Brian nodded. "Probably be an interesting journey," he remarked idly. "If we could actually see anything of it, I mean."

"Well, there might be time for sightseeing in the morning, depending on what time we all fall out of bed. The sooner we can get on the road, the better."

"I hope at least there'll be a bath," yawned Greta, "and hot water, wherever we end up staying."

"At this point," re-joined Allan wearily, "all I really care about is that there's a bed. I just want to shut my eyes and forget about the world for a while."

Which was a sentiment that seemed to appeal to them all equally, if the chorus of approving grunts that greeted it was anything to go by.

For an hour or so after this they ran along wide, well-lit, moderately busy roads, skirting a town which they were past almost before they knew it was there; no motion to turn back towards it was proposed, however, and they kept on doggedly in the belief that there would be somewhere suitable just around the next corner, or maybe the one after that. In the rear portion of the minibus people were either asleep or, like Dennis, sitting bolt upright with folded arms and blank minds wishing for it all to come to an end as rapidly as possible.

"We're heading too far north," said Brian, after a while. "We need to find a left turn somewhere and start going west again." He flourished the map, and Gus inclined his head slightly to glance towards it. "This road here, if we haven't passed it yet."

"All right." And within a further few minutes they had turned onto a smaller road, this time without lights but pointing in exactly the right direction, and when the houses on either side of it had thinned away to nothingness they found themselves in flat farmland, under a sky in which moon and stars were completely absent. Had it not been for the avenue of regularly-spaced trees, rising grey and stately like the columns of a cathedral, there would have been nothing between themselves and the horizon but the occasional thin triangle of a distant church spire. "This is fuckin' spooky," remarked Gus, as the pale shape of a horse in a field loomed briefly in the headlights and then was gone, and it began to be apparent that there were low-lying wisps of mist standing along either side of the road like silent wraiths. "Go on, or turn back?"

"Go on," declared Brian — unilaterally, as it happened, but none of the others spoke up against him.

For a while after that there was no sound beyond the thrum of the engine and the gentle jog of tyres on a cobbled surface, punctuated by the occasional disgruntled snore from the back seat. As the fog stole further and further over the road the van's progress slowed until it seemed as if they were driving through thick cotton wool, and the sounds of Allan's sleep grew steadily less contented; he could now be heard muttering indistinguishably from time to time, but the only word ever really recognisable was the infrequent exclamation 'no!' Clearly, whatever reality his dreams were presenting him with, it was a troubled one.

Dennis, in less sympathy with the man even than usual, hunched further into his seat and tried to imagine himself somewhere else, in a far more congenial setting, amongst people whose company he actually enjoyed. That would have been easier, perhaps, if only he could actually remember anything that was not this road, this trip, this group of people: Poland and the match seemed to have been an immeasurable eternity ago; England, further away still.

"This is hopeless," Gus murmured, almost to himself. "I can't see a bloody thing. At this rate it'd be quicker if we had a man out front with a red flag."

"I can scout ahead with a torch, if you think it'll do any good," offered Brian obligingly, but even he didn't sound especially convinced.

"Nice idea, thanks, but I think it would be too dangerous. If anything came along in the opposite direction you'd have had it before you knew where you were."

"All right. Although we haven't seen any other traffic for a while. It really feels as if we're out in the middle of nowhere, doesn't it?"

"Well, yes," Gus was obliged to admit. "But on the other hand, a road must lead somewhere – otherwise there'd be no point in having a road at all!"

As a piece of logic this was straightforward enough, Dennis conceded, but not altogether unarguable. There was still the nagging possibility, for example, that they were on a farm track or quarry road, and that they could find themselves fetching up unannounced at some Belgian farmhouse door and being chased off with a double-barrelled shotgun. Either that, or tipping over the edge of a quarry in the dark and not being found until the men turned up for work on Monday morning. Besides, Gus knew as well as he did himself that a road could still be there long after whatever it had once led to was gone. There were Roman roads all over Europe that started and ended apparently at random in the middle of the countryside, where every trace of the communities they had served had been swallowed up by time, and the road they were on now was beginning to feel like one of those – as if it somehow existed in isolation, outside time, and they were the only travellers ever to venture along it. He might even have suggested out loud that it was a sort of Flying

Dutchman of roads, except that he knew he would be shouted down by smart-arses in a hurry to remind him that they'd left Holland behind them hours before.

"Oh, fuck it, just stop this," said Allan, from the rear of the bus. "I mean it, pull up here for fuck's sake! It isn't safe to go any further!"

"What's the matter with him?" Brian turned his head to see what was going on, and so did Dennis; there was little detail visible in the seat behind, however, just a bundled figure lifting its head unquietly. Gary and Greta were stirring, and an unsympathetic murmur of complaint issued from their general direction.

"Nothing," pronounced Dennis, dismissively. "Just talking in his sleep."

"It's not safe," Allan insisted in the same quiet tone, half reason, half panicked insistence. "We need to stop right now!"

"Go back to sleep, Allan, and stop being a pillock." Really, it was difficult to take this sort of thing seriously; they had all had far too long a day already, they still had no idea where they were going to sleep tonight, and pratting about in Belgian countryside in the fog wouldn't be any sane person's idea of a good time.

"Yeah," drawled Gary, "just shut the fuck up, will you? Haven't we got enough bloody problems without that?"

"Let me out then," returned Allan, more urgently. "For fuck's sake, just let me out!"

Something in his rising agitation flipped a switch in Dennis's head; childhood trips in his grandfather's car, the one with the smelly red leather seats, and Dennis's obnoxious little brother sitting for hours at a stretch with his stomach heaving, clutching dementedly at the refuge represented by a plastic bowl. "Oh shit, I think he's going to be sick. Fuck it, Gus, we'll have to stop!"

Heaving a theatrical sigh of exasperation, Gus obediently stood on the brake; there was nowhere close at hand where they could safely pull off the road, which in any case was barely wider than the track of the Toyota's wheels, but the absence of other traffic should at least mean they would be all right where they were as long as they were relatively quick. "Dennis, open the door and let the bugger out; he's not throwing up in my bloody bus if I can help it!"

Dennis, galvanised into action, fumbled with the catch, pushing the side door open and allowing thick fog into the van's interior. It was cold, wet; it wrapped itself around their faces like the sticky tendrils of candy-floss.

"Come on you," he commanded Allan, "out! There's a nice big ditch out here; you can chuck up into that!" And so there was, six feet wide and full of shining black water, on the surface of which the mist was floating lightly.

Dennis virtually bundled Allan out shivering onto the road, pushed him out the way a jump-master pushes a reluctant parachutist; would have kicked him up the backside, too, if only their respective positions in the van had allowed it.

"You stupid sods, don't you understand? Can't you see what's happening? The bastards are waiting for us, further up the road!"

"What? Who are? You're not making any sense, you wazzuck; there's nobody waiting for us; nobody even knows we're here!" Which was not, now that he came to think about it, quite the comforting sentiment Dennis had been intending to impart, and far from calming Allan all he had really succeeded in doing was further disconcerting himself.

But Allan was too distracted to continue the conversation on any level, comforting or not. He was staring around himself wildly, as if trapped and desperately seeking an escape route. Then without preamble he turned and, taking only a couple of steps by way of a run-up, quickly leaped away across the drainage ditch beside the road and scrambled up the bank at the far side of it, his long legs carrying him off at high speed into the uncharted darkness of some anonymous farmer's field until he was completely swallowed up from sight inside a dense band of the all-enveloping wet fog.

"Oh shit," groaned Dennis, staring after him with his brain calcified into total inactivity and a sinking sensation in his stomach. "What the bloody hell are we supposed to do now?"

5

"Well, go on, Dennis," said Gus, after a long, stunned silence, "don't just sit there, do something!"

"You what?"

"You let him out," said Gary. "You go after him."

"I let him out so that he wouldn't puke in the van. How was I supposed to know he was going to run away?" Admittedly it was something a Labrador retriever might have done in the circumstances, but in a grown man it had been so far beyond the expected as to be utterly ridiculous.

"You didn't," acknowledged Brian, reasonably. "Here, you'll need this." He pulled a heavy-duty rubber-covered torch out from underneath his seat. "Don't lose it," he cautioned. "I borrowed it from my dad; it's got his name on it."

"Are you serious?" Automatically Dennis accepted the torch, and stared out through the open door towards the roadside ditch, the opposite bank, and the fog.

"Yes, I'm serious – why not?"

"Me. On my own." Dennis wondered if he was the only one who thought this suggestion at all strange. Apparently he was.

"Well, I can't go, can I?" asked Gus, reasonably. "I'm driving."

Brian only shrugged when Dennis's gaze returned towards him, and he knew better than to look in Gary and Greta's direction at all. Catch those two ever volunteering for anything useful, if they had the chance to laze around and moan about it instead! No, if anyone was going to embark on this foolish mission, it was undoubtedly going to have to be Dennis.

"Right," he said, jumping down from the van. "You lot just stay here, then."

"Can't," said Angus. "We're blocking the road. We'll find a place up ahead to pull over, and then we'll walk on back and meet you."

"Bloody typical." Dennis didn't have the energy to be annoyed with them. In fact, he was beginning to wonder why he'd ever been stupid enough to expect anything different in the first place. Instead he said, "I won't be long – I hope." After all, doing this sort of thing was a lot like having dental surgery; the longer you put it off, the worse it was bound to be in the end. Stuffing the torch inside his jacket and pulling the zip up to his chin, he took a couple of paces alongside the ditch, found the place where Allan had crossed it, and launched himself optimistically towards the far bank. He landed on all fours and scrambled to his feet, wiping mud from his hands onto the legs of his trousers. "Thanks a bunch, guys," he said, under his breath, before fumbling for the torch and setting off in the same general direction Allan had taken. Vaguely he heard the van's engine and the rumble of the wheels behind him, but he did not turn back towards it. Sometimes you were just on your own, and that was all there was to it; it wasn't as if he hadn't become quite used to the idea over the years, after all.

The land was as flat as a pancake, its surface soft and clinging underfoot. Within only a few steps Dennis found that the soles of his boots were becoming clogged with mud, but at least the softness of the ground made it possible to follow a set of tracks that he had to presume were Allan's; surely nobody but themselves would be mad enough to be blundering about in this particular part of the world on such an unpleasant evening? Whatever, he had a bloody good mind to box Allan's ears for him when he finally caught up with the bastard; there was only so much frustration and stupidity one man could take without snapping, and Dennis had been close to breaking-point before they'd even boarded the Turdo Ferry on the outward journey. Ever since, he'd been biting his tongue and giving vent to the occasional snide remark when what he would really have liked to do was haul off and smash Allan right in the smug rabbitty teeth and see what effect that had on him. Solving problems with violence never really worked, as Dennis knew all too well, but it didn't half make you feel better about it at the time.

In the meantime, however, he had a job to do, and unless he did it none of them would be getting out of this place tonight.

"Allan? Where the fuck are you?"

He had to repeat it several times before an answering cry reached him from somewhere in the darkness. Instinctively he turned towards it, aware of the stunted dark shapes of trees arising out of the mist and grateful for them; at least they would provide him with shelter and a landmark of sorts. Beneath his feet the occasional stumbled footprints had turned into a definite narrow path which he now followed, calling out again and again at intervals.

"Over here," he heard eventually, much closer than he had been expecting.

"Where?" Startled, Dennis almost dropped the torch.

"Here. Keep your head down, and be careful where you put your feet – there's a body just in front of you."

"A what?" Surely he must have misheard that part? Astonished, Dennis took a half-step sideways and felt his feet beginning to slither out from under him. His arms flailed as he tried to right himself, and he cursed under his breath as he lost control of his feet completely, and they and the torch went flying in opposite directions. In utter blackness he toppled over the lip of a hole he hadn't realised was there, falling onto something warm and yielding below, the wind knocked out of his body so comprehensively that he could barely struggle to his knees without help. As he floundered in the dark his hands encountered a solid shape covered by rough textile, to which they clung desperately and quite without understanding. It was better than nothing, he thought, and at least it wasn't moving.

"Easy," breathed Allan, unexpectedly close to his ear. "You're safe for the time being. Just hang on to me for a moment, 'til you get your breath back."

In total bewilderment Dennis did exactly that, hearing his own gasping with sheer incredulity; his heart was thundering as if he'd just run a marathon, his whole body shaking uncontrollably. It was ridiculous of him to have been so incapacitated by a simple fall; uncomfortable though it might be, good clean mud was really nothing to worry about it – would all wash off eventually.

"Shit, man, what the fuck … ? Did you say a body? A dead one, do you mean?"

"Yes," said Allan softly. "I think it might be Gary."

How absolutely typical of Allan, Dennis thought, to be so stupidly and unnecessarily melodramatic! "Don't be a wanker," he growled in annoyance. "I've just left Gary back at the van, as large as life and twice as bloody ugly."

"I know – but he's here too, Dennis, believe me. Look around you for a moment, eh?"

And there was something in the stunned seriousness of the tone that commanded his unwilling attention. Dennis ceased fussing about his own situation – about the injuries he might have sustained but hadn't – and instead raised his head and began to look around himself properly. The air was clearer here, the fog had gone, and the horizon line all around them displayed a light show bigger and more extravagant than the stage effects of even the most ambitious rock band. No demented pyromaniac genius could ever have conjured up this little lot; blasts of blue, red and yellow fire, thunderclouds of smoke, a massive bombardment of sounds that echoed loudly through the sky. With a demented scream a star-shell raged over their heads, bursting in mid-air like something out of a Guy Fawkes' entertainment – a bloody Brock's Benefit showing the whole of the surrounding countryside in clear, flat and perfect detail. It hung above them like a miniature sun, quite long enough for Dennis to realise several very important facts; that the minibus was nowhere to be seen, for example, and neither was the road; that the tediously smooth fields of Belgium for miles around them were torn and gouged and pockmarked; that the body resting at the lip of the hole was undoubtedly that of Gary Illingworth – and, with still more of a sinking feeling, that he and Allan were almost certainly not in Kansas any more.

The flare died away, and he clutched at the sleeve of the man he unequivocally knew to be Allan Ogilvie, but who didn't look very much like him – at least, not more than superficially. There were definite resemblances, but this man was younger, fuller in the face, and had short hair and a military moustache. And the reason for that, of course, was that he was wearing military uniform.

"Allan?" he asked, in some trepidation. "That is still you, isn't it?"

"Yes." But there was an indefinable difference about the voice; it seemed a lot less disillusioned somehow, as if it still had something it wanted to believe in.

"How can it be? You look completely different."

"So do you. You've got curly hair, for a start, and you can't be more than twenty-five years old."

"I'm thirty-fuckin'-seven," protested Dennis, grabbing for what he thought was one of the few established certainties in his life.

"Not here, you're not."

"Here?"

"Look around you," Allan repeated, almost whispering into a temporary lull in the bombardment. "Where do you think we are? Or maybe that should be 'when'?"

His brain still reeling, Dennis looked. Bomb craters and mud surrounded them, barbed wire and bodies; he didn't know what it was he had been expecting, but it definitely wasn't this. But for the fact that he could see no living human beings apart from himself and the man beside him, this could almost have been a battlefield of seventy-five years earlier.

"Fuck no," he swore fervently. "No way. This can't be what it looks like. It can't be here, it can't be … now. This your sick idea of a practical joke, Allan, is it? You arranged it all? Very bloody clever of you, I must say."

Allan weathered the tirade calmly. Too calmly, perhaps, on reflection. "Dennis, I didn't exactly arrange for Turdo Ferries to go tits-up, did I? And if they hadn't, we would never have been on this road in the first place. I didn't arrange the fog either, and I wouldn't know where to start organising a fake battlefield. Besides, have a look at yourself and tell me what you're wearing – or did I somehow manage to arrange that, too?"

"Well, I … "

"What?"

Jeans, leather jacket, big thick sweater, England scarf, woolly gloves. That was what Dennis should have said. That was what he had been wearing when they left the hotel this morning, and what by all logic he should have been wearing now.

"Uniform," he said instead, flatly. "Battledress, gaiters, boots, gas cape."

"Rifle, bayonet, helmet," Allan completed for him, knowingly. "Wear that lot to the match last night, did you?"

"No, I didn't." And, dully, there was the sensation of being divided, of being two consciousnesses trying to occupy the same limited amount of space. On the one hand there was the bright image of a hospital corridor, of Dennis in his fitter's overalls changing light bulbs and replacing locks, but behind it as though in a secret compartment there was a rural Northumberland childhood, plough horses, a little apple-cheeked grandmother with an accent you could cut with a knife; that was not Dennis's real childhood; those were not his own memories.

"You do still remember the match?"

"Poznań? Lineker equalising in the 77th minute? Bloody Austrian referee? 'Course I do, but … " He looked around him at the ruinous landscape. "So where are the others? Brian? Gus? Greta?"

"How the hell do you expect me to know that?" demanded Allan. "I got here just a few minutes ahead of you, and the only other person I've seen was Gary – and he was already dead when I arrived, I think. When I woke up on the bus I knew – God knows how, but I knew it somehow – that the Germans were going to be shelling this road. I knew we were all going to end up in the middle of it somehow, and all I could think of at the time was finding a way to keep you safe; just don't bloody waste time asking me why, all right?"

"All right." And in truth, there was a part of Dennis that would really rather not know – a hidden aspect of himself that had occasionally wondered if his total antipathy towards Allan wasn't somehow a symptom of the opposite, an extremely reluctant attraction to the man. He'd always loved and hated in exactly the same place, for reasons he'd never quite been able to fathom, as if all strong emotion looked exactly the same to him and he'd never quite managed to distinguish longing from loathing. "So you're seriously tryin' to tell me that this is exactly what it looks like? The First World War? How the fuck can it possibly be? I wasn't born until March 1954 and you were … what?"

"February '49."

"Right. So, at least thirty years after this lot finished, then. Which means this can't be the real bloody First World War and Gary can't be bloody dead, either. He was perfectly fine when I left him on the bus. Well, fine for Gary, anyway."

"In 1991," Allan reminded him gently. "You left him in 1991. It doesn't make sense to me, either, Dennis, but at least I can prove that it's a real bloody battle," he went on, shakily determined, "and I can't say I care a lot which one it is."

"Prove it? What d'you mean, you can prove it? How?"

"How? Because I'm bloody wounded, that's how! I've got shrapnel all the way up one leg and more in my fuckin' chest. Gary must've stepped on a shell or something, I suppose; he caught most of it, but I got the rest." He paused, clearly waiting for the importance of his words to sink in. "I don't know if I'll be able to move from here on my own, Dennis; I'm afraid you're gonna have to help me."

"Move?" repeated Dennis, stonily. "If you're right and this is a real war, I'm not bloody moving anywhere!"

Sighing, Allan pulled off his cap and ran a hand through his short fair hair. "Have you by any chance got a cigarette?" he asked, plaintively.

Dennis fumbled in his pockets and brought out a paper packet containing two Senior Service, plus a box of matches. They concealed the cigarettes in their palms as they lighted them, after which Dennis dropped the used match into the water at the bottom of the shell-hole, where it fizzled and went out. Allan inhaled deeply, coughing as the sharp warm smoke hit his chilled lungs.

"Listen, I reckon I've got this figured out," he said, with a firmness Dennis hadn't noticed in his voice before. "What we have to do is look for the path we came in on and follow it all the way back to the road. The others should still be there waiting for us, shouldn't they?"

"Oh, right, it's gonna be that easy," groaned Dennis. "In the pitch dark, through all that hate, to a road that may not be there when we get there, a bus that hasn't been built yet and people who won't be born for another thirty years?"

"We don't know that," Allan told him, with a shrug, "but what we do know is that the longer we stay here the weaker I'm gonna get. This is real shrapnel in my leg, and I'm bleeding real blood – and those fuckin' whizz-bangs overhead are real enough to kill us if they hit us, no two ways about it. So what d'you want to do, Dennis, sit here and wait 'til they get our range? Or were you maybe hoping to be rescued? Only I don't see a lot of people about, do you, and personally I'd rather try to keep moving. What about you?"

"Yeah," said Dennis at last, accepting the scenario at face value and recognising the merit of action – any kind of action – over inaction. "I bloody well would, an' all."

"Okay. Now, I can probably walk, if I can lean on you a bit, but there's no way I can climb out of this hole all on my own; you'll have to get out first and pull me up. Grab hold of that tree root for leverage."

No sooner was this suggested than it was done. Amid flashes of lightning and a deafening roar from the heavens, answered by occasional pinpoints and crackles from the wood behind them, Dennis managed to pull himself back up out of the pit and lay flat, face down in the mud, his head and shoulders extended over the rim of the hole. A moment later Allan's arms were warm around his neck and he was pulling Allan towards him, horribly intimate but somehow completely appropriate, one hand reaching down to grab the belt at the back of Allan's greatcoat. With a twist and a gasp he found that he had taken the man's full weight – not massive in itself, but encumbered by heavy uniform and a considerable quantity of mud – and wrestled it over, out of the trap, and safely onto the flat Belgian clay.

"Christ," whispered Allan. "Thanks for that, mate."

"You're welcome," Dennis breathed, as soon as he could. "What should we do about the body, do you think?"

"Push it into the hole." Then, in response to Dennis's appalled silence, "Well it won't make any difference to him now, will it? Here, I'll give you a hand."

Allan crawled round, pushing the corpse towards Dennis. Dennis grabbed it by the shoulders, supported its weight as Allan shoved the legs around, then let it slide slowly over the rim and down into the base of the muddy pit. By the intermittent light of the bombardment it was just about possible to make out the torn face of their comrade turned sightlessly towards the sky, and now Dennis could be in no doubt whatever about the identification.

"Cheers, Gary," he said, reaching down to pat him on the shoulder. "He was a bit of a tosser, you know, but he wasn't a bad mate for all that."

"Well, if this works out the way we're hoping it will," replied Allan in a tone of great sagacity, "you should be able to say that to him yourself in a few minutes' time."

6

"Do you reckon there's any chance of finding the torch again?" asked Dennis, hopelessly. He had been reaching around him where he lay, patting the ground, examining by touch objects that he could not see.

"I didn't realise you had a torch. What happened to it?"

"I dropped it, when I fell into the hole. Didn't you see it?"

"No, but then I couldn't even see you until you'd virtually fallen in on top of me. Is it important?"

"It belongs to Brian's dad. I'll probably be in serious shit if I've gone and bloody lost it."

"Considering the situation we're in at the moment," replied Allan rationally, "being in shit for losing a torch seems a minor inconvenience. Besides, if it's a 1991 torch, how do we know it would even work here?"

Dennis was about to reply that it had been working, right up until the moment when he dropped it, but he thought better of it. He was learning – and quickly, too – not to take anything for granted in this altered reality. Whatever he had imagined was logical and true about his life before this evening, that was clearly no longer the case; he had left 1991 carrying a torch, walked across what had seemed to be perfectly ordinary field, and found himself in an earlier decade – or so it would appear. That being the case, he supposed, all bets were off; nothing could be relied upon any more, nothing was even remotely certain.

"Hold it." Allan had also been reaching around himself and exploring their surroundings with his hands. "Here's something that might be useful."

"The torch?" Dennis hadn't given up hope of finding it, whatever Allan said.

"No, but I think … I think it could be duckboards – and they wouldn't be here for no reason, would they? They must lead somewhere; if we follow them, they might take us get back as far as the road."

Dennis slid round to Allan's side, almost swimming through the mud, reaching out along Allan's arm to locate the object Allan's hand had found. "Yeah, I think you could be right." He rolled over, sat himself upright on the duckboard, made a few experimental movements to determine how far the surface extended, how safe it was, and in which direction it would be likely to take them. "It goes off that way," he said, pointing out across the shallow landscape. The bombardment had eased somewhat, or at least it had moved away from their location temporarily, but the price they were paying for this respite was drastically reduced visibility; there was smoke hanging in the air, and they could see very little further than they could reach. "Here, I'll help you up."

Taking it slowly, he somehow eased Allan up onto his one good knee, supporting him underneath the arms. Then he levered himself to his feet, and in the same ungainly movement pulled Allan with him, shaking alarmingly, and brought him in tight against his shoulder where Dennis could support the weight of both of them. The cry of agony that issued from Allan when he tried to put his wounded foot to the ground was muffled against the thick collar of Dennis's coat.

Dennis's arm tightened around his waist. "We'll have to do this like a three-legged race, I think," he said, attempting to sound calm and in command of the situation. "When I move my right leg, you move your left and vice versa. Start out on your left."

"Okay, Dennis." Allan's unwontedly meek agreement indicated, more clearly than words, that he was in pain and holding himself together with extreme difficulty and only by the force of sheer persistence.

"Right then, off we go. Left … right … left … right … that's the way … "

For the first few paces Dennis dictated every movement, taking Allan through it step by step as though trying to coax a rusty robot, until at last a rhythm was established. Allan was struggling, however, that much was evident; every time his weight fell onto his injured leg there came a hiss of pain from between his tightly-clenched teeth, but somehow he managed to keep going, far longer and far more determinedly than Dennis had ever expected he would. Obviously he'd made the elementary mistake of misjudging this man, who was unquestionably a right royal pain in the arse in most ordinary situations; give him a real trial to bear, however, and it became apparent that there was quality in him; Allan clearly had mettle which his everyday life just never allowed him to display, that was what it was. Nevertheless with each step forward Dennis continued to praise him, muttering incoherent sounds of encouragement as he would have done to cajole a dog or a horse, and steadily it did seem to get easier. The solid duckboards carried them slowly across the mud, the sounds of shelling retreated into an unimaginable distance. Then there was a sudden and absolute silence, in which Dennis's quiet words were the only sounds that could be heard at all.

"Hush, man, we're nearly there, it's all right now, lean on me."

A biting cold wind cut through them, and Dennis heard the familiar sound of his boots hitting first a little wooden bridge and then a metalled road surface; not Army boots, either, but the comfortable old hand-made hiking boots he'd had for years and which he'd been wearing this morning when they set out from the hotel in Berlin. He stopped abruptly, looking up in bewilderment into Allan's face; older, thinner, wearier, framed by wispy fair hair that was decidedly not of military regulation length.

"Can you see … ?" he asked uncertainly, battling the disorientating sensation that reality had shifted once again and that the man leaning against him in such unaccustomed intimacy was none other than his constant and wearying nemesis from the medical imaging department. The bloody, torn uniform had gone completely; Allan wore a dark polo-neck, a padded jacket, a warm scarf, and an expression of utter distress and confusion.

"You look like you again, Dennis, and I … I think … I feel as if I look like me."

"You do," confirmed Dennis. He wanted to unwrap his arm from around the man's waist quickly, before Allan got the wrong idea about him, before anybody saw them like this, but bizarrely he felt as if it would be far too pointed a gesture after all that they had shared. "Are you okay?" he asked instead. "How's your leg?"

"Still fuckin' painful – but it isn't bleeding any more, thank God!

I think I've probably sprained my bloody ankle."

"I'm not surprised," growled Dennis. "Fuckin' about in Flanders fields at this time of the soddin' night, man, honestly, I ask you!"

"I know," was the amiable response. "Would it help if I said that I was really sorry?"

"It might," acknowledged Dennis. "A bit." Still puzzled, however, he reinstated his hold, accepting Allan's weight back against his shoulder, and guided him a few steps further along the road. "Can you see the minibus at all?"

"I'm not sure," Allan told him, squinting through the gloom. "Are we even going in the right direction?"

"Yes. There was only one ditch, so as long as we keep it on our left we'll be heading the right way. They said they'd walk back along the road to look for us, as soon as they'd found a safe place to pull over."

"They," Allan repeated, thoughtfully. "Will 'they' include Gary, do you think? And if so, will he be all right?"

"Presumably," replied Dennis cynically. "He was all right when we left him, wasn't he? If you want my opinion, I think he'll be absolutely fuckin' marvellous."

"Well then, if so, who was it we buried in the shell hole, and how can he possibly be in two places at once?"

Which were both very good questions indeed, acknowledged Dennis, and he would certainly have liked to have the answers to them himself, but he had come up with an even better one of his own. "More to the point," he said, "what the fuck were we doing there in the first place, and who exactly were we anyway?"

Allan stopped in his tracks, turning awkwardly to face Dennis. They could barely see one another in the darkness, but his hand went briefly to Dennis's shoulder and patted it with rough but genuine affection.

"Two people who met by accident in the middle of nowhere and came to care about each other," he answered softly – and his voice, when he spoke, was that of the younger man, the officer Dennis had encountered in the isolated shell-hole some seventy years ago or more. "You'd been separated from your unit and I'd been abandoned by mine. You saved my bloody life out there, Dennis, and I have no intention of ever bloody forgetting it; you do know that, don't you?"

"I think so. I think I can even remember some of it. I got you out as far as the road, didn't I, and then something happened … "

"Well, for fuck's sake, will you look at this little lot, then?" From out of nowhere, Gary's uncouth tones cut through something that could almost have been magical, a closeness that belonged to another time and place keeping two men who cordially disliked one another welded together as if each was the only thing in the world the other really cared about, as if they could never bear to be more than a fraction of an inch apart.

"Gary?" Trotting footsteps were approaching along the road as they loosed their mutual hold.

"Who else? Not interrupting anything, am I? Only I never knew you two were that way out! Gonna have to lend you that German porno mag I found; lots of kinky ideas for queers in there, you know."

"Don't be such a fuckin' pillock," spat Dennis, aggravated beyond belief to have been interrupted at what had seemed to be an important and pivotal moment. It had evaporated utterly in the instant he spoke, all that nebulous awareness of one another, only to be replaced by ordinary pedestrian awkwardness and embarrassment. "Allan's sprained his ankle, he can hardly walk on it."

"Not a bit surprised, bounding off across the field like a scared bloody rabbit," responded Gary, from a position of imagined superiority. "Must be out of your tiny little mind to do a thing like that. You do realise, don't you, that there's still unexploded ordnance in some of the fields over here? This is where they fought the bloody First World War, you know, you moron!"

Dennis and Allan exchanged glances, sharing an instant of rueful unity. No, there was no way in the world they could say anything about what had happened to them without appearing to have gone completely round the bend and come half-way back again. In fact, it was something that could never really be discussed with anybody else at all, and scarcely even between the two of them; whatever it was, whatever it had been, it would just have to remain unacknowledged.

"Well," said Allan, "in that case we got off lightly, didn't we?" And

Dennis noted with relief that his breathing was easier, and that he straightened up almost gratefully as if he was glad to have shed the injuries he had been carrying back there in the past. His hand still remained on Dennis's shoulder for balance, but otherwise he had fully unwound himself from their grudging half-embrace, and Dennis could not help experiencing that as some kind of unaccountable loss.

"I'll get Gus to back the van up, shall I?" Gary volunteered, making almost his first useful contribution to the journey so far, but before he had gone more than half-a-dozen steps towards his objective the sound of an engine coming to life cut through the stillness of the night. As the minibus drew closer, trundling backwards along the road, the pool of light it brought with it illuminated limitless flat hectares of neat cabbage rows and corn stalks, across which the mist now lay in slender ribbons. It showed up also a walled enclosure a hundred metres away on the opposite side of the road, standing dark and silent and dominated by a Cross of Sacrifice, within which thirty or forty identical white grave markers stood in immaculate serried ranks.

"What the ever-livin' fuck is going on with you two?" demanded Brian testily, reaching them a moment later. "Are you on some kind of pills or wacky-baccy?"

Allan shrugged. "It's nothing," he said, relinquishing his hold on Dennis and struggling fully upright at last. "I had a nightmare, that's all. Claustrophobia. I get that sometimes."

"You might've said something before," admonished Brian. "Scared the living bloody daylights out of all of us. What've you done to your ankle?"

"Sprained it, I think. And I'm sorry to say I've lost your father's torch."

Dennis stared at him. Allan hadn't even admitted to seeing the torch in the first place, and now here he was spontaneously taking the blame for losing it! They really must have stepped through a doorway into an alternate dimension, somehow, if Allan was going to start behaving altruistically for a change.

"Bloody lucky you didn't end up steppin' on a minefield, if you ask me," said Brian, taking Allan's arm and steering him solicitously towards the minibus. "Gary reckons people still get blown up here on a regular basis; he said that was probably the way we'd end up finding you – follow the boom and the flash of light, and don't forget to bring a plastic bag."

"Charming," observed Allan, drily. He was pulling himself in through the open side door of the minibus, reaching for the refuge of his seat, draping his blanket back around himself. Dennis could fully sympathise with that; he was bloody cold, too, as well as bloody tired. Time travel, whether real or only illusory, had turned out to be a peculiarly exhausting occupation.

"Right," said Angus, as the others boarded and arranged themselves in their usual seats. Brian slammed the side door vehemently before scrambling into the front. "Can we proceed, do you think? Only I wouldn't mind a wee bite of something or other to eat, if we can find a place somewhere still open; my stomach thinks my throat's been cut."

"There's a village," said Allan, with new – or perhaps it was old – certainty. "Couple of miles up the road; we might find somewhere to stay there as well."

"Oh aye, right, we're gonna take the word of a man who goes walkabout in a minefield for no apparent reason, are we?"

"No," said Dennis suddenly, "he's right, there is a village. You'll see a turning for it, a mile or so further on."

"And you know this how? Did you maybe find an all-night tourist information office right out there in the middle of the field or something?"

"No." But inspiration had struck Dennis completely out of the blue, and he was learning that such things must never be distrusted. Besides, Allan had gone out on a limb for him by deflecting Brian's anger, and he felt it was up to him to make some sort of contribution of his own. "There was a signboard about the Battle of Torville Wood, and there was a map on it. There's definitely a village; I'm surprised we can't see the lights from here, actually."

"Oh aye," shrugged Gus. "All right then, we'll give this village of yours a try, shall we? And just make sure you watch out for the low flyin' pigs along the way."

"Assuming it's safe to go up the road at all now?" asked Gary, glaring back pointedly to where Allan was rubbing his injured ankle and grimacing.

"I've already apologised for that," said Allan, sullenly. "It wasn't intentional, but I suppose you're going to make me go on paying for it anyway, aren't you?"

"Just as long as I possibly can, mate, yes," replied Gary. "Pure bloody comedy value, you are. Or would be, anyway, if we weren't already all so fuckin' tired."

"For fuck's sake, Gary, give the poor bugger a break," growled Dennis, becoming thoroughly sick of the whole business. "He said he was sorry; how much more d'you want out of him?"

"Oh, I see; joined the fan club, have we, Dennis?" The tone was insultingly snide and patronising.

Dennis looked up sharply and caught Allan watching him, a thoughtful and somewhat sheepish expression on his face, and shuddered involuntarily in reaction to it. There was obviously more to this situation than met the eye – and what met the eye had been peculiar enough already, so whatever was to come would presumably be stranger still. Plainly it wasn't anything like over yet, anyway, whatever it was, because something had changed that could not be unchanged; the magic lamp had been smashed to smithereens and the genie had escaped.

"No," he answered, slowly. "I haven't joined anybody's fan club, Gary, and yours least of all. But I don't actually think we should be trying to punish people for stuff they can't do anything about, do you? You might as well have a go at him because he's tall or blond or because he's a Hartlepool supporter or something."

"Is he? A bloody Hartlepool fan?" This last suggestion seemed to have acted like a catalyst on Gary; Allan had always kept very quiet about his club allegiance, if he had one, so Gary fastened onto this completely random suggestion as if it had all the seriousness of holy writ. "You're a 'monkey hanger', are you, then? Explains a lot about you, that does, come to think about it. A bloody 'monkey hanger', of all bloody things."

Allan shrugged off Gary's disgust. "I might as well be," he conceded. "Yes, if you like, I'm probably a 'monkey hanger'. I'm sure there are worse things than that to be in the world, aren't there?"

"Not many," replied Dennis. "Not if you happen support Darlington like Gary here."

"Ah, well, in that case, clearly, I'm the lowest of the low."

"Yeah," said Gary, turning back to face the direction they were travelling. "That was actually the conclusion I'd already come to, believe it or not."

7

The village that Allan and Dennis had so confidently foretold turned up precisely on schedule. Scarcely more than a junction of three roads with a marketplace attached, it announced its presence with bright street lights and the blare of rock music issuing from a small corner café as they passed it, driving into a cobbled square which had a fountain at the centre and also boasted three or four barred and shuttered shops. In front of one of these, an *épicerie-tabac*, Gus drew the minibus to a halt and switched off the engine with an air of finality.

"I'm not driving anywhere else tonight," he said. "If we're moving on from here at all, Dennis can drive; three countries in one bloody day is enough for anybody."

"Yeah, well, this is nothing but a fucking little shit-pit," responded Gary morosely, "although I suppose we might be able to get a drink at that place on the other side of the square. C'mon, Greet … "

"Hold it," said Brian, from the front seat. "We need to sort out somewhere to stay before we can think about anything else. Anybody got any ideas?"

For a moment or two they all looked at one another vacantly, not a thought of any value among them, and then at last Dennis shrugged and pointed towards a narrow street, not well lighted, which ran away from the corner of the square and was swallowed almost immediately by a sweeping curve. "Let's try down that way," he suggested, apparently quite arbitrarily.

"All right, then, that way it is."

They descended from the vehicle in a bunch, taking their luggage with them. The chill evening air cut through them all as they waited for the van to be locked up before moving off; Gary's half-hearted suggestion that someone – presumably himself – ought to stay there and guard the luggage had been ruthlessly shouted down on the basis that if any of them had to go trudging around rural Belgium on a cold night, then they all

51

bloody well had to suffer equally. Besides, they were all acutely aware that anyone who wasn't consulted when the accommodation was arranged would be bound to take every opportunity of complaining about it afterwards, and nobody wanted to give anyone even the least smidgen of an excuse for doing so.

"Why is it so fuckin' quiet around here?" asked Allan in confusion. "Does everybody go to bed the minute they've had their tea, or something? Isn't there anything decent on Belgian telly at this time on a Friday night?"

Indeed, most of the houses that fronted the square were either fully dark or showed lights only on their uppermost storeys; it was not a massively welcoming environment for the casual visitor, and Dennis could sympathise entirely with Allan's protestations; the place was making him feel uncomfortable too, and it was difficult to put his finger on precisely why. It all just looked wrong somehow, that was the only thing he could think of – and yet the Coca-Cola signs, the smart new SAAB parked nonchalantly on the pavement, the graffiti favouring Standard Liège, all of those were perfectly ordinary and consistent with the location. His unease, therefore, must stem from another source – perhaps from a memory of what this place had been when he had visited it in that other, shadowy life. Despite himself he shuddered at the notion; he had somehow been hoping that having walked away from the battlefield and driven a few kilometres down the road might have shaken something loose, might have freed him – and Allan too, for that matter – from the disquieting effects of their recent experience, whatever it might have been. He wanted it to be over and done with, for fuck's sake; he wanted those images out of his head; he wanted not to have to think about Allan on any level at all beyond the superficial; he wanted to be able to go back to disliking him with a clear conscience if he possibly could, and he had the distinct impression that in this case the feeling was unequivocally mutual.

"This is a world class bloody bog-hole," muttered Gary, "and it's closed!"

"Oh, I don't know." Brian sounded rather more insouciant than usual. "I reckon you could probably have quite a good time here, if you only happened to know the right people."

"Oh aye, absolutely," confirmed Angus, playing along. "Plenty of birds and booze to be had on every street corner, I'll be bound – although just at the moment I'd be happy to settle for a wicked-strength double chicken vindaloo with extra poppadums."

"Yeah, well, this is Belgium," returned Gary, "and right in the middle of fuckin' nowhere at that, so I'd say you're probably gonna be bang out of luck."

Even this fractious discourse, however, had dwindled to nothing by the time the travellers drew level with a pair of decorative wrought-iron screen doors on the front of a tall, anonymous house. There wasn't a light showing anywhere in the place, but a small hand-written card in the window bearing the single word 'Chambres' had stopped them in their tracks.

"That's 'rooms'," said Greta, "isn't it? 'Shombrers' – bedrooms, right?"

"Rooms," repeated Brian, thoughtfully. "Anybody want to give this place a try?"

"I don't know, man, it looks fuckin' closed to me." Gary was clearly in one of his more negative moods this evening – as, indeed, when was he not?

"If it was closed, they would have taken the card out of the window," put in Allan, sniffing disdainfully. "Not exactly rocket science, is it?"

"Well, we're not going to find out anything standing here, are we?"

Taking the initiative, Brian stepped forward and pulled enthusiastically on the bell rope. A distant, silvery note rang somewhere deep in the bowels of the building, and for a long moment afterwards there was complete silence – so long and complete, in fact, that they were almost beginning to turn away before there came a small sound of movement from within and Greta cried out, "There's a light!"

There was, too, although not a steady electric light – something flickering and uncertain, accompanied by shuffling and extremely elderly-sounding footsteps.

"*Qui est-ce?*" asked a querulous voice from beyond the door.

"We're English," said Brian, ignoring a grunt of Caledonian protest from Gus. "*Nous sommes anglais.* We're looking for rooms. Six of us; three twins or three doubles would do, if you've got them. *Trois chambres.*"

"*Moment*!" An arthritic fumbling with keys, and then the wooden door opened and a woman who seemed to be well over eighty years old, carrying an oil-lantern of similar vintage, peered out at them through the viney tendrils of the elaborate wrought-iron grille. She seemed to look them all over very thoroughly, and then said – in careful, but clearly rusty, English – "No rooms double; six rooms single I have. One thousand and eight hundred francs."

"One thousand eight hundred?" Gary was clearly about to go into orbit. "That's thirty fuckin' quid! You can get a really good room in a decent hotel for less than half that, with a minibar and everything!"

"You can if you can find one," Brian reminded him patiently. "And I, for one, am considerably past caring at this point. *Merci beaucoup, madame*, I think we'll take it – won't we, lads?"

But the old lady seemed perturbed. "No," she said, worriedly, the hand with the key in it gesticulating as though to halt a runaway horse. "*Pour tous.* One thousand eight hundred for all. Bed, *et le petit déjeuner.*"

"Bloody hell, that's cheap! Thirty quid for all six of us, for the night – in single rooms?" Changing direction faster than a shoal of fish, Gary repeated the old lady's words back to her, as though to be absolutely certain she understood what she was saying. "Are you absolutely sure about that, missus?"

Her confidence in her English – or at least her ability to make herself understood – seemed to be returning gradually, however, and she nodded vigorously and smiled, holding up the oil lamp by way of explanation. "No *électricité*," she told him, almost conspiratorially. "Cheap, because no *électricité.*"

"Oh, right! Well, that sounds like a bloody good deal, then, doesn't it?"

"Language, Timothy!" exclaimed Greta, elbowing him firmly in the ribs.

"Right, yes, sorry. I meant 'it sounds like a very good deal'. So, what do you reckon, fellers? We'll have some of this, then, shall we?"

Receiving several nods of approbation in response, the old lady applied the key to the iron gate and it swung open slowly, after which she stood back to admit them all to a darkened hallway in which all they could make out clearly was a tiled floor and the looming shapes of some extremely large furniture. However a moment later their hostess had taken a spill from her lantern and lighted a gas lamp on a bracket above a side-table, presenting them with a dog-eared register which she invited them to sign. There were also numerous candles in holders standing there ready for the use of her visitors.

After they had completed the formalities and Brian had handed over the money, the landlady steeled herself for a further speech.

"No keys to rooms," she said. "You choose any – *elles sont toutes les mêmes.*"

"The rooms are all the same? So it doesn't matter which ones we have? There are no other guests, then?" Brian concluded. "Nobody else staying here?"

A shake of the head was the only response to this question.

"Brilliant. We'll go off and have a bit of an explore, then, fellers, shall we? This way?"

"Hang on a minute," put in Gus. "Do you know anywhere where we can get something to eat this evening?" he asked. "I know it's late, but does that place in the square maybe … ?"

They all watched, fascinated, as the old lady made the double translation – first out of Gus's Scottish accent into English, and then from English into French.

"I have … *ragoût* … with shicken," she suggested, somewhat tentatively. "*Les repas sont inclus.* In the kitchen; *une demi-heure.*"

"Included in the price?"

"Yes. *Inclus.*"

"Good God, that's incredible! Er, I mean … " Gus faltered, and it was clear to Dennis that he had only just noticed the crucifix the woman wore around her neck and the larger and more elaborate one hanging in a prominent position on the wall – right next to a sign boldly proclaiming *Défense de fumer.* There would be no smoking in the bedrooms, then, and whatever else this place might be it was obviously a

Christian household. Out of respect, therefore, it would be probably be a good idea to hold back on the blasphemy a bit, just for the duration of their visit. "You're a princess, Madame ... " Gus continued, enthusiastically. "A princess, that's what you are."

Which produced an indulgent laugh from the old lady, who pointed at herself and inclined her head politely. "Duclos," she said. "Madame Duclos."

"Aye, well, *vous êtes une princesse*, Madame Duclos." And to judge from the delighted reaction to this unconventional utterance, it would appear that Gus was well on his way already to becoming the landlady's favourite lodger.

It did not take long after that for the travellers to choose six single rooms, widely distributed over the central two storeys of the house. They wandered around for some little time carrying their candles, looking into the small, narrow rooms, each with its identical single bed neatly made and topped off with a heavy brown blanket, its identical washstand supplied with ewer and basin. There were a couple of bathrooms, too, fully fitted-up with plumbing which was ancient but in essentially good order, everything clean and fresh but standing apparently unused for some considerable time. On the first floor the bedrooms all led from a wide common area arranged as a library or classroom, with a big central table flanked by wooden benches as its dominant feature and bookshelves lining the walls. From here a staircase like a ship's ladder took the more adventurous to a second landing which housed more bedrooms and another bathroom, from which again a further staircase headed off towards the loft.

After only perfunctory perusal Dennis selected a room at the back of the building, which looked out over a long, narrow garden, the details of which were completely obscured from view. His cream iron bedstead lay half-blocking the window, but by squeezing himself into the remaining foot or so of space and pressing his face up against the glass he could just make out a faint red glow somewhere in the distance; someone was smoking in the garden, which probably meant that it would be all right for him to do so too. There was the faintest sliver of a moon overhead, showing itself intermittently between the heavy clouds, and he could not help being reminded by it of his brief but surreal experience of the war, the shell-hole and the body at the lip of it, and of the man who both was and also most emphatically was not Allan Ogilvie.

They had followed their counterparts' instincts in finding this place, nothing could be more certain than that. This particular house, to judge from its looks, must have been here long before the First World War, and had plainly endured whatever panics and alarms that dreadful fracas had inflicted upon it. Arranged as it was, with all these little bachelor rooms and large communal areas, it would probably have made decent accommodation for officers just a little way behind the front line, although whether they had actually lived here and gone to the war every day – just as in civilian life they had taken the Metropolitan Line to their offices in the City – or simply fallen back here occasionally for rest and recuperation, he could not begin to guess. What he did know, however, was that he would never have seen the inside of the place himself in those days; he was squarely NCO material, he had no illusions about that, but Allan … yes, Allan was an officer all right. Was, or had been, or something like that …

Wrapping his arm supportively around Allan's waist and helping him out across the duckboards to the road had only been the beginning of the story, as far as Dennis could remember it. He had some sort of vague recollection of helping him into the back of a providential ambulance, handing him over with relief into the charge of a one-eyed driver and a Quaker boy with pimples who looked far too young to be out in the middle of this mindless chaos without his mother, but beyond that there was nothing; whatever had happened next, he had no memory of it. This was a dangerous bit of road, too, and not even an ambulance was guaranteed to pass safely along it; admittedly the Germans usually respected the red cross symbol, but there were numerous tragic tales of them not doing so – either through inadvertence or through downright deliberate malice. Maybe that had been the last time he'd seen Allan, in that other life. Come to think of it, maybe that had been the last time he'd seen anything at all.

When he closed his eyes now, he could see it again; Allan's face looking back towards him as the ambulance doors closed. He hadn't been alone in there, either; there had been six of them on stretchers in the back and Allan sitting on the floor, plus the driver and the boy in front. A direct hit on that, and they were all nine of them in their coffin already – a mobile coffin, too, making its way slowly over the gashed and rutted road surface, its only slight protection from attack the emblem painted on its sides and roof.

Dennis passed a hand slowly across his face, shuddering uneasily at the recollection. A man alone in the middle of a German bombardment might just as well have taken out his own pistol and shot himself through the head, his chances of survival were so slim – yet there he had been nonetheless, watching as the ambulance moved off along the road, and he had made no move to seek cover whatsoever. Had he maybe had a death wish? Or had he just become so used to the extraordinary that it no longer had any meaning for him? Either way, his life expectancy wasn't going to be spectacular unless he made some attempt to take cover, but still he didn't move; still he stood, watching the ambulance depart, feeling as if something massively important was ending before it had even properly begun.

But it isn't over, is it? he realised, putting the pieces together only slowly in his mind. *It isn't over, and it can't be over, because we're here again. Because there's something we still have left to do.*

And, whilst that was not a thought which gave his present-day self any comfort whatsoever, the deep-down remnant of the lonely soul who had stood so still for such a long time on the Menin Road was virtually singing an aria of rejoicing.

8

"I absolutely love this place," enthused Brian as they assembled, half an hour later – this time minus Greta – in the large ground floor kitchen of the guest house. "I've been exploring. There's a massive garden, and up in the roof-space they've even got their own chapel."

Gus, parking himself on the bench beside him, elbows on the wide plank table, grinned conspiratorially.

"Are we gonna have to say a prayer, then, before we eat?" he asked, grabbing a hunk of bread from the basket and tearing it apart in a shower of crumbs.

"I don't think so," Brian reassured him. "Apparently this used to be a soldiers' hostel, a long time ago. They stayed here when they came out of the line or just before they went back in. I don't think religion was ever compulsory, even in those days – just available for anyone who wanted it."

"How d'you know all that, then?" Gary, also taking a piece of bread, seemed to forget what it was for and instead used it to illustrate his question.

"Been talking to Madame Duclos," was the dismissive response. "She says she used to get a lot of English visitors through here at one time – that's why she had this leaflet printed." He produced a garish little number on shiny paper. "Since the war they've had a Catholic summer school here every year, and the rest of the time they run it as a sort of convalescent home for overworked priests."

"Which war?" asked Allan, quietly. It was almost his first contribution, having maintained an uncommunicative silence since they'd reconvened.

Brian paused in his tracks, seeming to consider for a moment. "You know, that's a good point – she didn't actually say, but the way she talked about it made it sound as if she'd been here at the time. She couldn't have meant the First World War, though, could she? I mean, she'd have to be … what, at least ninety-something?"

Half-unconsciously they all turned and looked across to where Madame Duclos, oblivious to the subject of their conversation, was ladling stew out onto plates. She was humming to herself quietly under her breath, clearly lost in her own little world, and there was a smile of great contentment on her face – a hostess who was apparently only fully at her ease when welcoming guests. Well, she was pretty good for ninety-odd, but ninety-odd she might well be; none of them was particularly disposed to doubt it.

"Hey, you did tell her Greta wasn't coming down, didn't you?" Gus asked, nudging Gary with his foot. There were six plates on the kitchen counter.

"Oh, fuck, no, I didn't; my French is crap. Brian, you tell her, will you?"

"Mine isn't all that wonderful either," returned Brian. "I got my 'O' level, but that's about all – and that was a long time ago." Nevertheless he got to his feet and walked across to speak to Madame Duclos. "*La jeune femme ne descenderas pas pour le dîner,*" he said. "*Elle ne va pas très bien.*"

"*Oh, Monsieur, a-t-elle besoin de quelque chose?* Does she need … something?"

"I don't think so, Madame, thank you … Gary, what was it you said was up with her? Migraine?"

"*My*-graine," Gary over-corrected. "It came over her really quickly, poor cow. *Mal,*" he added to Madame Duclos, pointing to his own head, "*à la tête.*" He did not seem to realise that he had raised his voice.

"*Ah, oui, je le comprend; ma sympathie.*" Their hostess pushed away the empty plate, and instead distributed the pot of stew amongst the remaining five.

"So you do speak French, you pillock," said Brian, resuming his seat and glaring at Gary.

"Not a lot. Just about enough to get a girl into bed, really. '*Voulez-vous coucher avec moi, ce soir?*' Doesn't necessarily work in other situations, though."

"And probably best avoided here," put in Dennis, wryly. "Although she looks a game old girl, so you never know."

"*Trés amusant* that, Dennis," Gary shot back, his Yorkshire accent making it "Trezz amuzont."

"Careful," said Gus, quietly. "Time to change the subject." His bushy eyebrows waggled warningly in Madame Duclos's direction. "Anyone up for a raid on that café place in the square, after we've eaten?"

"Not me," said Dennis. "I'm for an early night – and anyway, you want me to drive in the morning, don't you?"

"Yes, it'll be your turn," supplied Gus. "You get us as far as the ferry, I'll take over again when we get to the other side."

"Right then. In that case, I'm definitely gonna need my sleep. You lot can go ahead without me this time."

"Lightweight," accused Gary, sounding thoroughly disgusted with him.

"Soft southerner," Gus corrected, with a grin.

"Well, I'm afraid you'll have to count me out as well," said Allan, and it seemed to Dennis that they were very carefully not looking in one another's direction. "I've been tired all day, and everything aches; and I think I might be sickening for something."

"You're sickening all right," Gary told him, with more than a hint of malevolence, but that was the moment at which Madame Duclos approached the table with a large tray held high, set it down and proceeded to dole out plates of chicken casserole, and as usual the prospect of food drove all other considerations from the minds of the travellers and they settled to their meal with enthusiastic and very well developed appetites.

By the time they had finished, it had been decided that Gary, Gus and Brian would jointly attempt an assault on the café they had passed on the way in, and which their hostess had assured them would still be open. Madame Duclos provided a set of keys for the front door and the iron gate, entrusting them to Gus with an enjoinder not to lose them, please, for they were older than he was – and in their bustle and enthusiasm to get going and to sample the local Belgian beer none of them paid very much attention either to Dennis or to Allan. Nor did the two of them pay very much attention to one another, for that matter. In fact, even before the others left, Allan had disappeared upstairs again and Dennis had wandered out into the garden to find a quiet place to smoke a cigarette before turning in. Once outside, however, he found that it was not quite so dark as he had been expecting; there was some ambient light from the backs of the nearby houses, and the mist – already far less heavy in the small town than it had been out in the countryside – was higher and lighter now, with the moon occasionally showing through it. Nonetheless he carried his lighter, and there were a few looming landmarks that he could follow – a high wall on the right-hand side, against which fruit trees had been trained, parallel with which ran a gravel path, and further down the projecting timbers of what appeared to be some sort of pergola or gazebo, which would be roughly where the person he had seen smoking from the window must have stood.

Reaching the structure, Dennis flicked his lighter and was able to make the tentative identification of it as a species of pergola. There were roses growing up one side, leafless but recognisable from their thorns, and another climbing plant growing up and tangling with the roses but at this time of year nothing but wiry stems – and he was no gardener, anyway; a plant was a plant to him, and he had never needed to know much about them at all. However he felt comfortable enough here to lean back against one of the upright pillars, apply a flame to the tip of his cigarette, and inhale slowly, at long last allowing himself to see some of the pictures that had begun to seep in around the edges of his consciousness.

This garden had not always been a decorative one, he remembered that very well. The shelling had not missed it completely, with stray shots landing from time to time in the flower beds, and when the Padre had originally taken the place over and turned it into a combined monastery, sanatorium and clinic he'd set the more ambulant of his visitors to growing vegetables to supplement their rations. With the help of an occasional Other Rank, the convalescent officers had over a period of time barrowed in horse-manure from the baker's stable, piled it in one corner to rot down … and, several months later, their replacements had forked the rotted muck into the beds. Apart from the Padre himself, there hadn't been one man left alive of those who'd planted the seeds by the time it came to harvesting the crop.

Glancing up at the building, Dennis could easily make out the window of his own room, with the moonlight reflecting on the glass. Beside it the shuttered window would be Greta's, and there was one other on the floor above. Gus, he knew, had opted for a room at the front of the house overlooking the street, but he had no idea what accommodation the others had chosen. Nevertheless he had the strong conviction that this must be Allan's window, simply because it looked out in the same direction as his own; that just seemed to be the way this phenomenon was operating somehow, keeping himself and Allan apart from the rest of their group either physically or psychologically and throwing them together into close proximity. He didn't entirely like the way he felt that this was heading, either; the mixture of attraction and repulsion was almost more than his brain could process and remain coherent – which, he supposed, was just about right if he seriously considered that he was temporarily two people, one of whom apparently wanted to spend a great deal of time with Allan, preferably in intimate circumstances, and the other of whom couldn't really stand him at all. In any event, it was about time there was some kind of resolution of whatever it was that was going on between them; he could feel himself being pushed – or steered, perhaps – towards something which he both wanted and feared, and he had little doubt that he would probably have experienced the reality of it for himself before the night was over.

He'd made a point of never fully acknowledging it, but there had been the occasional moment in his life when he'd been assailed by not-exactly-heterosexual emotions. At school, after puberty hit, he and a bunch of other boys had regularly polished Percy together; playing with yourself for the benefit of an audience was generally considered good, clean, dirty fun in that crowd, with those who came most often or most copiously attaining almost heroic stature. Dennis himself had come three times in one lunch break, and for a little while after that he'd been held in considerable esteem around the school – right up until the first of their group had actually managed to put his inside a girl, and after that no other such achievement would ever be quite so good again. And Dennis had been a late developer, too, when it came to girls, largely because he didn't fancy any of the ones at school who were desperate enough to fancy him; he wasn't looking for a long-term relationship and he wasn't looking for a wild party, either, so when it came to sexual relief he was quite happy to go on using his own two hands, simply because it was the least complicated of the available options. When eventually he'd lost his virginity to a girl she'd made all the running, had him a few times, and then dumped him, and that had been the pattern ever since. He wasn't hugely enthusiastic about women as a species, really; he got on better with men, on the whole, although so far very few of them had appealed to him sexually either. He'd never ruled it out completely, but he wasn't going to go looking for it because that would just mean that he was queer. No, if it was ever going to happen, it would just damned well have to come looking for him, that was all.

And now, of course, it was beginning to look as if it had.

The truth of this became literally apparent when he heard the almost stealthy sound of footsteps approaching him along the gravel path. He looked up in their general direction, but the moon had escaped again between the clouds and he could make out little in the almost total darkness that surrounded him. He had no doubt, however, who it was, and the thundering of his own heart increased until it was suddenly louder and more percussive than any enemy artillery barrage.

The figure was not hurrying, as though as reluctant for the encounter as he was, and he made no attempt to step forward to greet it; he was half-afraid that it would be Allan, and half-afraid that it would not, but when it came clearly into view no room remained for any doubt. Hands in pockets, thin shoulders hunched against the cold breeze, Allan stepped through the entrance to the rose arbour and stood quietly beside him, staring out towards the black indistinctness of the garden.

"Dennis," he said at last, with no inflection whatsoever.

"Hello, Allan."

A cold enough greeting, considering the heat of the emotions that roiled between them.

"Have you got a cigarette?"

That same calm question, the one which had been asked and answered in a muddy shell-hole with only a dead body for company.

Dennis fumbled for his packet and handed it over. Allan took one. The match in Dennis's hand flamed into life and Dennis reached over to light it for him, looking up as he did so into the shadowed face of his younger companion from no-man's-land. They were between worlds again, he realised; this man was both Allan and not-Allan, and Dennis could read in his eyes everything he had ever wanted to see in the eyes of a lover – intense lust, possessiveness, an almost desperate desire for him. Slowly Allan's fingers curled themselves around Dennis's wrist, holding him steady, supported his shaking hand, his fingertips sliding softly into Dennis's palm. Not without considerable difficulty, for the two of them were suddenly as nervous and uncoordinated as virgins, Allan's cigarette was eventually lit and the match was dropped. Allan, however, did not release his hold on Dennis's upraised hand, retaining it and stroking it lightly long after the little flame had been extinguished.

"It's you, isn't it?" Allan said at length, raggedly. "You, from the shell-hole."

"Yes." The noticeable difference in the sound of his own voice was no longer any surprise to Dennis, he was quite literally not entirely himself at the moment. "I've been waiting for you."

"I know. I'm sorry, it took me longer to get here than I thought it would."

"Aye, well, at least you're here now. How's your leg feeling?"

Allan shrugged. "It's not giving me much trouble at the moment," he answered, striving for a lightly conversational tone. "It aches a bit in the cold weather, that's all. You know how grateful I am for everything you did."

"Well, you could buy me a pint some time," suggested Dennis, managing despite himself to make the words sound almost casual. He threw down his cigarette onto the gravel path, grinding the embers beneath his booted foot, unwinding his body into a weary stretch. "If you don't object to being seen drinking with me, that is."

"I don't object personally," Allan informed him, "but we're not the only ones we have to consider, I'm sorry to say. Other people wouldn't like it very much if we were seen out drinking together."

"Aye, well, bugger other people, it's none of their bloody business, is it?"

"I wish it wasn't," said Allan, "but I'm very much afraid it is." And a sullen silence fell for a short while, after which he continued, more carefully still. "Look, if you'd like to come up to my room, I've got some red wine tucked away. Not half as good as beer, obviously, but if you don't mind making do ... well, we could let our hair down a bit together, and just see what happens afterwards."

The slyness and the deliberate *double-entendre*, together with the fingers that still stroked and tickled the palm of his left hand, combined to send a frisson of sensation rushing through Dennis's entire body.

"And what, precisely, is it that you've got in mind?" he asked, aroused aggression colouring his tone. His hand closed tightly on the delicate fingers, crushing them. "Tell me what it is you're wanting from me, up there in your room."

"Don't be so fuckin' stupid, Dennis," was the somewhat dismissive response. "It should be bloody obvious what I want, and it's exactly the same thing you want – you and me, a night, a bed, no worries and no regrets. Nobody will ever know about it but the two of us, so don't you dare try to pretend to me that you don't want it just as much as I do."

And, when he put it like that, Dennis suddenly became aware that perhaps he was not the only one for whom this was a less than attractive – although still compellingly necessary – proposition; Allan wanted him and didn't want him, too, in equal proportions.

"Where is your room?" he asked. It was all the acknowledgement he was prepared to make, at this stage, of the power of Allan's argument.

"Second floor, last door on the left – next to the bathroom."

"All right. You realise do that if I get caught, though, they'll throw me out and probably court-martial me? I'd have to pretend to be a burglar or something."

"I know. But better to go to prison for that than for buggery," Allan reminded him, quietly.

"I'd rather not go to prison for anything, if it's all the same to you." Now that it was decided, Dennis was feeling considerably more relaxed

– almost enough to be mildly humorous, in fact.

"Well, you know the solution to that then, don't you?" replied Allan, squeezing his hand fiercely and then loosing it again before stepping back into the darkness of the shadowed garden. "Just don't go getting yourself bloody caught, all right?"

9

"Wait a minute." It had taken a long time for Dennis's brain to kick into gear and catch up with the speed of events, and Allan was already moving away from him. He was reluctant to let him go, however, before they had settled one more thing between them. "There's a condition."

"Oh?" A chilly and less than encouraging syllable.

"Yes." It was almost too late to say this, but Dennis was determined not to enter into anything under false pretences. "Look," he began, slightly grudgingly, "it's just going to be one night, okay, and then we're going to forget about it for the rest of our lives. I mean it; no trying to trap me into anything long-term."

Allan turned back towards him, casting down his cigarette. His hand stole slowly around the back of Dennis's neck, stroking the short hair above his uniform collar, and he leaned in to rest his forehead against Dennis's. Dennis could smell the mustiness of trench life on his clothing, could taste the cigarette smoke on his exhaled breath.

"I'm not planning to get pregnant and force you into marrying me," Allan promised, clearly. "Although it could be a lot of fun trying."

Dennis let out a long, slow, sigh of relief. "That's what you want then, is it? That way round, I mean?"

Allan seemed to consider for a moment before replying. "Well," he said at last, "I could go either way, I suppose – but I do have a preference, yes."

"Right." Allan's arm was languid around Dennis's neck and Dennis felt himself being pulled closer all the time, Allan's mouth lifting to his. "I get the message. I can do that."

Closing, Dennis kissed him without any remnant of uncertainty, recognising the willingness with which Allan opened to him and accepted his probing tongue as an earnest of the entire body's response to a more intimate possession. On some level Dennis had always known Allan wanted him – that they wanted each other – although he'd been extremely reluctant to admit it. It was scarcely as if they considered themselves friends in everyday life, after all; in fact they didn't like each other one little bit.

This was very different from everyday life, however, and this was not simply Dennis Patterson from Hunmanby and Allan Ogilvie from Hong Kong and Catterick via York; there were other people who were involved here also. Allan's irritating shallowness and Dennis's pathetic inhibitions belonged to another life, one that was of supreme irrelevance here. It was the man he had rescued from the shell-hole by the Menin Road that Dennis held in his arms now; the comrade met by night in no-man's-land, desired almost from the very first moment of their meeting.

Unconsciously he let the kiss become more aggressive, poured into it all the frustration he had felt since their original untimely separation. They had both known what they wanted virtually within seconds – some electrical spark had flashed between them which had little to do with who they were in that insubstantial future and everything to do with the reality of being two soldiers in a battle zone, who might die within minutes and who wanted a little comfort from each other first. All over the Western Front there were men who, before an action, turned together with busy hands and mouths; it had been extremely serendipitous to have found one another at all, and was even more so that they had a bed and a whole unbroken night to themselves.

The kiss ended, and Allan's heart thudded against his own through multiple layers of thick uniform; he was as breathless and fluttery as any gentle girl, clinging to Dennis as though to the only rock in a stormy sea. Dennis squared his broad shoulders and eased free of the importunate hands.

"Go on up to your room," he said. "I'll follow you."

"You're sure? You're not going to run out on me after all this?"

"I'm sure. I said we'd do it, and we'll do it – come hell or high water. I promise."

"We'll do it this time, because we didn't before?"

"Yes," confirmed Dennis quietly. "We'll do it this time, because we didn't before."

Progress through the garden was frustratingly slow, but eventually they reached and pushed open the back door, stepping into the house precisely as they remembered it from all those years before. There was nobody in the kitchen, and they slid past it softly into the wide hallway; this, too, was almost completely dark, with only the single gas lamp – turned down as far as it would go without disappearing altogether – lighting the whole area. They paused at the foot of the carved oak staircase.

"There's somebody up there," Allan breathed. There was in fact the faint glimmer of a lamp in the general area of the education room; someone up late studying or writing letters, no doubt, which was always easier to do in the communal areas than in the monk-like cells that were the individual rooms. "I'll try to distract whoever it is while you slip past." He did not wait for an answer, but instead squared his shoulders and clattered briskly up the staircase, as though deliberately seeking to attract attention to himself.

"Ah, Padre, good evening, I see you're all alone," he said, just a little too loudly for verisimilitude. "Are you working on a sermon?"

"Good evening, Captain." The accent was exactly what Dennis had been expecting to hear, familiar as he already was with the benign cadences of the West Coast of Scotland. "Nothing so elevated, I'm afraid; this is *More Fragments From France*, the new Bairnsfather book. Would you like to look at it?"

"I'll read it over your shoulder, if you don't mind," suggested Allan. Dennis saw him stepping away from the staircase and crept slowly up after him, being careful to remain in shadow. He knew, however, that from a certain point close to the top he would be able to look through the bannisters and take in the whole room at floor level without being seen himself – assuming nobody in the room was looking directly towards him at the time, of course. One step after another, slowly and almost without sound, he eased himself higher until he could see that there was nobody in the education room but Allan and the Padre, and they both had their backs towards him. Nevertheless it wasn't difficult to imagine the Padre's kindly face – his twinkling blue eyes behind the round-framed gold spectacles, the jovial pepper-and-salt beard which often, even at the most inappropriate moments, seemed to be unsuccessful in concealing a cheery smile. There were few men in the world as uncomplicatedly friendly as this particular Padre, and there were a great many individuals on the Western Front who had had cause to be grateful to him before now. Nevertheless, the Christian faith was very firm upon certain matters, and Dennis was sure that the Padre knew his Leviticus as well as any other man of the cloth; *if a man lie with mankind as he lieth with a woman, both of them have committed an abomination: they shall surely be put to death, and their blood shall be upon them.*

Then again, this Padre was not a fool; he would have been no fit man for his job if he had not been well aware that sometimes, through adversity, men fell into a closeness which the Church considered abominable. Whether or not he suspected it of them in particular, however, Dennis had never known, and was not especially keen to discover now; he did not want to be on the receiving end of the man's opprobrium, or even of his sympathetic disappointment.

Allan was crowding the Padre, leaning over him in a way that was so intimate as to be almost oppressive, making it difficult for him to turn around even if he heard a sound. This was all Dennis needed; despite his heavy boots he was able to move quietly across the floor, his movements masked by the riotous laughter Allan seemed to have manufactured out of nowhere in response to one of the drawings.

"Ha!" he was saying, cheerfully. "I think I had that little round-faced chap in my unit at one time; I remember his horribly mutinous expression only too well!" And then Dennis's feet were on the steep stairs to the next level and he was moving as quickly as he reasonably could, under cover of Allan's bravura performance.

The upper corridor was in full darkness, but here Dennis was on more familiar ground; he knew the layout of the building well enough, having been in and out of it on numerous errands. He could not be here as a resident or a guest, certainly, but he was considered good enough to carry out the occasional menial maintenance chore when his other duties permitted. At any rate, there was nowhere much for him to go wrong here; one hand on the wall would keep him going in a straight line, and all he needed to do was move silently until he reached the room beyond the bathroom, right at the end of the corridor.

The bathroom door stood open, so that was easy enough to identify. Beyond it was only one door, closed, and Dennis slipped through that soundlessly, leaving it ajar, waiting in the darkness. There would be a view out to the garden from here, too, if the shutters were not fastened, and further beyond the garden to the horizon where there was still the occasional flash and flare as something went off, something fell, some objective crumbled, some other life was ended. There had been a time when he would have felt all this most acutely, and worried about it too, and been concerned for the men shivering beneath the enemy barrage, but he had long ago learned to reserve his energy, his pity and his anger, for situations he might possibly be able to influence himself. Out there on the battlefield other people were in command, other people were making the decisions and moving their pieces about as though on a giant chessboard, and Dennis knew he had no choice in the matter but to do precisely as he was told, immediately he was told it, and try his hardest not to complain about it.

That was out there, though, and for the time being he was in here, making his own decisions – such as they were – well away from the focus of the conflict. He was on weekend leave; he could spend it as he chose. Many men preferred either to get riotously drunk or to find themselves a willing sexual partner somewhere, and to do their best either to father a little half-Belgian child or to catch some socially unacceptable disease or other, but Dennis's predilections were entirely different. Dennis sought instead to quench his unfulfilled desires in solid, masculine flesh, whatever the Bible had to say to the contrary, and he had never yet quite managed to feel guilty about making arrangements to do so.

Confident footsteps were approaching along the corridor, and the door was opened and shut very firmly. For all that there were no actual locks, these little apartments were provided with bolts on the inside so that their occupants would be sure of being undisturbed whenever they wished it.

"I don't particularly want to light the lamp," said Allan, barely above a whisper but matter-of-factly for all that. "Will you be able to manage?"

"I expect I will. Some things are better done without light, anyway."

"True. *The unfruitful works of darkness*, and so forth. If we open the shutters, we should just about be able to see what we're doing – as long as we remember to close them again before morning."

"All right, then." Dennis shrugged, then remembered that the other man probably couldn't see what he was doing. He moved lightly across the room, finding and drawing the bolt on the shutters completely by touch, and pushed them open to allow the delicate silver vapour of starlight into the room, subtle as perfume, touching lightly upon bright surfaces such as a button, a wristwatch, or the gleam of an eye.

"Why don't you take off your coat?" whispered Allan. "There's a chair just behind you; try not to knock over the jug and basin on the washstand."

Dennis took off his cap, his greatcoat, and then the tunic of his uniform, putting them all down carefully in order on the chair. If trench warfare had taught him nothing else – and it had taught him a great deal, one way and another – then he had fully absorbed all the lessons about how to undress in the darkness so that one could find one's clothing in a hurry if necessary. Not that he often bothered to undress, out there in whatever dugout he found himself in; sometimes he'd take off his cap, boots and greatcoat, but that was generally about all. Disrobing completely, especially at this time of year, tended to be reserved for the occasional bath or medical examination and nothing else. He sometimes wondered whether they had all forgotten what they looked like under their uniforms, or whether indeed there was anything under the uniform at all.

Allan had also taken off his coat, cap, boots and jacket and was sitting on the bed, reaching into the little bedside cabinet.

"I think an expert would probably call this a deeply uncultured claret," he offered, apologetically. "It's a pre-war red, and that's just about all I can tell you; I bought it from someone in the village who was moving out and couldn't take it with him. You're the visitor, so you can have the glass; I'll drink out of the bottle."

The delicate operation of pouring wine in near-total darkness was accomplished with no great difficulty. Dennis held the glass still, Allan's hands folded around his, and then the mouth of the bottle was opened and the liquid splashed. Most of it seemed to have ended up in the glass somehow, as far as he could tell.

"Well, your very good health," murmured Allan. "Or should I say 'bottoms up'?"

"Yes, 'bottoms up'!" Dennis could not quite suppress an undignified chortle, which actually surprised him as indicating how relaxed he was, although he had scarcely expected to be. He sipped the wine experimentally at first – 'uncultured' was a very good adjective for it, in his opinion – then swallowed the remainder with increased enthusiasm. It was raw but vigorous, strong enough to guarantee a perfectly hellish hangover in the morning, but for the time being it conveyed a warmth and power for which in the circumstances he could only be wholeheartedly grateful.

He moved towards Allan, glass in hand, and reached to loosen the knot on Allan's tie, extracting the thing carefully and finally throwing it as far away as he possibly could. It was necessary to set the glass down to deal with Allan's collar-stud, but he accepted a silent swig from the bottle by way of compensation. Then, without finesse, he polished off his glass of wine and began to unfasten the buttons on his vest, economically pushing down his braces at the same time. Allan reached up as though to help him, but Dennis did not have any time for that; he tipped Allan back onto the bed and a moment later was on top of him, meeting Allan's mouth with his own and devouring it, this time also allowing his hands to roam freely over the slender body and slim hips, swamping Allan beneath a stronger and more dominant masculinity and grinding against him as though determined to come now, come hard, and forget about it all as soon as he possibly could – and Allan, still half-clothed, was eager and accepting beneath him, grinding back against his passionate thrusts, not remotely interested in sensitivity or finesse but demanding and giving in equal measure, desperate for some form of quick surcease.

It was over in seconds, the torrid urgency abated, the two men pulling apart in discomfort and something that felt obscurely like shame. It should have been nothing like so quick or so frantic when they had a whole night at their disposal, and if this was to be everything then it could surely only be described as disappointing.

"Oh, god, I haven't gone off as fast as that since I was seventeen," groaned Allan, close to Dennis's ear. "I hope you're going to stay and let me make it up to you somehow? Take the rest of your clothes off, maybe?" Not precisely an instruction; more of an invitation, really.

Dennis stood up, finished unbuttoning his uniform trousers and climbed out of them carefully. "These are going to need sponging in the morning," he said.

"Mine, too." Allan was wriggling out of his where he lay, before sitting up and draping them over the rail at the bed's foot, his shirt immediately joining them. A moment later he had also slithered out of his drawers and lay quite naked, his thin chest heaving. The smell of sex was already powerful in the room between them, and as Dennis discarded his underwear and stretched his whole body, flexing muscles he'd forgotten he'd ever owned, it was readily apparent that their adventures were not yet over for the night.

Allan reached out, taking Dennis's half-hard member appreciatively in hand.

"Want me to suck it for you?" he asked, guilelessly.

"You can later," Dennis promised, his own large hand going to Allan's groin, his fingers exploring elegant length and satisfying weight. "Wasn't there something you wanted me to do for you first, though?"

"Yes, please." A hoarse whisper. "From behind, and as hard and deep as you possibly can. Don't keep anything back; give me absolutely everything you've got. Make me forget the world. You can do that, Dennis, can't you?"

Climbing onto the bed behind Allan, stretching out body to body, stroking down his silken flank, Dennis settled a hand on Allan's slim backside and dug his fingers in possessively.

"Oh yes," he said, "I can do that. It's just what I've been waiting for." His free hand twisted a nipple, as Allan's fingernails raked back across his buttock.

"Then fucking well stop messing about, Dennis," demanded Allan urgently, "and just get on and bloody do it."

10

"You've done this before, I suppose," Dennis said, trying to make it sound casual.

"I have," confirmed Allan. "Not recently, though. There's no need to be nervous, anyway; I've got some Rowland's Macassar in the drawer – it's made from palm-oil, I believe, so it ought to be suitable."

The bedside cabinet was the cheapest, flimsiest imaginable, and the effort required to open the drawer was almost enough to bring the whole thing crashing down. Wrestling with it did little to increase Dennis's self-esteem, but when he did get his hands on the small bottle and took a deep breath before opening it he felt his confidence beginning to return. The contents didn't smell particularly good, but then he supposed that wouldn't worry either of them too much.

"You won't need a lot," Allan told him. "It goes quite a long way."

"All right." And really, when he thought about it, this part of the process shouldn't be difficult for a practical man like himself, one who claimed to be an engineer; it was in essence a simple enough process, a piston moving within a cylinder, and as such it could not reasonably be expected to function without lubrication. That was the way he decided to approach the matter, therefore, using all the care he would have used on the most sophisticated of mechanisms, carefully oiling all the moving parts and then delicately fitting the machinery together. The feeling of satisfaction was just the same, too, as he took his first slow plunge into the receiving body, all in one smooth and unencumbered movement.

"My God," said Allan, quietly, "that's good." In the circumstances Dennis was astonished he had retained the power of speech at all, if the sensations assaulting him were on a par with those he was experiencing himself; in fact the man either had a gift for understatement or he was much, much too used to this, because suddenly 'good' seemed too meagre a word, too pale and under-powered. No, this wasn't only good, it was of a different order altogether; it was grand, it was sensational, it was well beyond the power of words to encapsulate.

"There now," he whispered, soothingly. "We're going to make this work, between us, aren't we?"

"I'm sure we are." The sharp-boned backside pushed back against him, Allan's fingers grabbing him and pulling him deeper. "But you're definitely going to have to get moving some time soon."

So get moving he did, plunging and withdrawing slowly at first, like a reciprocating engine, converting movement into power and power into work, every thrust meeting its equal in resistance, friction creating heat, energy being transferred and applied. It was beautiful the way all this had been designed, he felt; the simple elegance of the mechanism doing exactly what was required of it with nothing wasted, nothing extraneous, just the straightforward giving and receiving of pleasure. And because it was so smooth, so absolutely faultless, it ran on without interference for a much longer period than he had ever expected it would, until in the end it was he who began to stutter and speed up, aware of a massive increase in pressure which urgently needed to be discharged. By the time it ran through his mind that perhaps he should issue some kind of warning it was already too late; he had completely lost the power of speech, and shortly afterwards he could no longer sustain a coherent thought that did not involve pushing again and again into the tight sheath that held him. There was a cry – though where it came from, he couldn't say – a gasp, a muddled whimper of regret, and then a valve opened and his entire system, as it seemed, drained abruptly into the containment vessel. A few more limp and exhausted thrusts and he was done with the whole process, collapsing onto Allan's back, sweating, gasping, his senses reeling and a chaotic kinetoscope dancing brightly through his mind.

"Fuck," he said, at long last; his first real attempt at language for a while.

"Well, yes, it was," came the amused response. "And I get the impression you're rather good at it, aren't you?"

"Am I?"

"I'd say you were, myself. I can't imagine nobody's ever told you that before."

"Oddly enough, no, they haven't." The very idea of his previous partners paying him compliments on his technique was risibly alien; they had hardly been the most articulate of individuals anyway, and Dennis had never expected them to consider him any more than merely adequate.

"Well, then, they were all idiots," came the crisp response. "Honestly, I can't imagine why you haven't been snapped up by someone a long time ago. If it was up to me, I wouldn't let you slip through my fingers – but it isn't up to me, I'm afraid."

And that, Dennis supposed ruefully, was the nub of the problem. They were emphatically not their own men, and that being the case there was very little chance of their ever having the opportunity to be each other's.

Some hours later the bombardment, having lifted in the evening, began again in earnest. Dennis detached himself from Allan's embrace, scooted down in the bed and looked out across the garden. All along the horizon-line gun positions were opening up, yellow fire hanging ominously above them. The business of the war had recommenced in full measure, and their hiatus from it was coming to an end.

"I'm afraid I'll have to leave you before too long," Dennis told him quietly. "I'm expected. You know how it is."

"Yes, I do." A defeated whisper. "But I'm glad we were able to have this."

"So am I." Allan changed position to join him where he sat looking out of the window, his arms draping languidly around Dennis's stockier frame. "How are you feeling now?" he asked.

"Strange, actually. I keep thinking that I should feel guilty, but I can't really seem to summon up the energy. What about you?"

"Well, I'm a bit sore, of course," replied Allan, a smile evident in his voice, "but otherwise wonderful. I always expected you to be good in bed, you know; in fact, the very first time I set eyes on you I remember thinking to myself, 'that man's definitely got something I want to get my hands on'." These words were followed by an extremely lewd chuckle. "And I did, didn't I, in the end?" he continued, wickedly.

"So you did," replied Dennis. "So you did. So when exactly was the first time you saw me, then?"

"The time you saved my life, of course – when you helped me out of the shell-hole. We should probably have talked about all that sort of thing before this, I suppose, but there just never seemed to be a chance. I never understood what you were doing all the way out there in the first place, for example."

Dennis shrugged. "Oh, it wasn't all that interesting," he said, dismissively. "I was just checking telephone wires. Your forward OP had been cut off, if you remember? I was sent under cover of darkness to see if I could find out where the line was broken, and join it back up again if possible. I never actually found the break, though; I was still in No Man's Land when the shelling started up again, and the next thing I knew the forward OP had taken a direct hit and been wiped out completely, so there wasn't any point in going on. I'd turned back, and I was trying to find my way back to the lines to ask for more orders, when I ran into you."

"Fell over me, more like," Allan corrected, wryly.

"Tripped on a tree root," amended Dennis. "I had no idea there was even a shell-hole there."

"Well, if it was a completely random accident, then it was a lucky one for both of us; if you'd only been a couple of yards to the left or right, or a few minutes earlier or later, we'd probably never have met at all. As it was, at least you gave me a second chance; you got me out as far as the ambulance. Otherwise I would just have died where I was, and nobody would ever have been any the wiser. I don't think I've thanked you for that yet, have I?"

"No thanks necessary; you would have done exactly the same." But Dennis was silent for a long time after this. "My memories of the next part are a bit hazy, though," he confessed. "I can't really remember where I went afterwards, or anything I did."

"No," admitted Allan, "neither can I – and, to be perfectly honest, that's the bit I don't really want to think about too much; there's a gap where those memories ought to be, and I'm not too sure I want to know why." He stopped, and then seemed determined to change the subject.

"Listen, is there any of that wine left?"

"Not much." Dennis was somewhat surprised, but grateful for the alteration in Allan's mood. "It's been open all night, too, so it'll probably taste like vinegar."

"It didn't taste all that good when it was fresh," Allan reminded him, "but my mouth's dry, and I don't really want it to be – only I seem to recall that you promised to let me suck you off, and after all there's no time like the present!"

The tone of voice, as much as the words themselves, went directly to Dennis's groin. If he was completely honest with himself, he hadn't regarded that particular promise with any degree of seriousness; the notion that anyone, least of all a man, would want to take him in their mouth and service him in that way had always seemed bizarre and incredibly distant to him, something that simply wasn't likely to happen. It happened to people in German porno mags all the time, of course, but they were also the people who dressed up in rubber or leather, who liked to be chained and whipped, and who had, on the whole, a far more interesting sex life than his own; such things didn't happen to ordinary blokes from his pathetically unglamorous walk of life at all. Besides, he'd imagined himself to be pretty well spent out and exhausted; he'd already managed a performance he hadn't expected to be capable of, so vigorous and enthusiastic that he was surprised there hadn't been complaints from the neighbours about the noise. Then again, maybe anyone who was used to trench life was also used to sleeping through a barrage of miscellaneous cries and thuds in their immediate vicinity, and certainly nobody seemed to have taken very much notice of them – although Dennis doubted they'd been as quiet as all that.

"Well," he smiled, "a promise is a promise," and wriggled back up the bed to plant himself flat on his back with his legs spread and his knees raised, in a posture of supine vulnerability and invitation. "Feel free," he offered, grinning lecherously into the darkness.

"Thank you," replied Allan. "I believe I will."

He took another mouthful of wine, then leaned down to set the bottle on the floor and positioned himself carefully, his long-fingered hands pushing Dennis's thighs apart until the strain on muscles and sinews was just this side of unbearable. Then there was the sensation of a cool, wet mouth, like the brush of damp leaves across overheated skin, sucking slowly on Dennis's testicles, at the base of his prick, and then rising in a complex pattern of slick tongue, sharp teeth, sucking, blowing, to trace coldly across his over-sensitized tip. It danced there briefly, exploring the slit, then took him into itself completely and tightened on him.

"Oh my fucking God, you've got me in your fucking mouth ... " Dennis wasn't sure whether it was the sensation or the forbidden – 'dirty', his Puritan upbringing insisted – nature of the act itself that he found the most powerfully erotic, but all at once and suddenly it was so close to being overwhelming that his instinctive reaction was to try to push Allan away from him. He only succeeded, however, in disrupting his attempt to establish any kind of rhythm; Allan merely paused and looked up, but otherwise remained in position. Only his eyes seemed to move at all, and there might just possibly be a faint expression of enquiry in them – although it was equally likely he was imagining it.

"No, it's all right," Dennis told him. "It's good, it's great – I'm just not used to it, that's all. Go slowly, all right? Slowly, or you'll lose me." And could that perhaps be an edge of panic in his tone? He wouldn't like to think so, but unfortunately it was all too possible; he was completely out of his depth here.

A grunt of assent, a slight nod of the head, and then Allan returned to his task, moving slowly and sensuously, and after a while Dennis began to feel confident enough to join him in it, to move against him in counteraction, to balance with him in thrust and withdrawal until eventually he almost began to believe that he was the one in control of the situation. Tentative, awkward, he placed his hands on either side of Allan's head, not so much holding him in place or guiding him as fixing on a single point of reference in the maelstrom, making sure he had something he could rely on when the waves of coloured light swept through him, when the star-shells exploded in the sky behind his eyes, when he spilled himself far beyond the point of dehydration into the all-accepting mouth. Not for nothing had this sometimes been referred to as 'the little death', this complete numbness and limblessness, this utter disorganisation of brain and body; Dennis slumped back, drained, his hands loosing their hold, his mind fragmenting with pleasure. There were things he should be worrying about, he knew, but they belonged to another world that was not here; all that mattered to him at the moment was the sheer gloriousness of the sensation in which he revelled, and the exquisite care with which it had been bestowed. Perhaps, after all, there actually were lovers who were prepared to put their partners' needs first – he had always believed there must be, somewhere in the world, although he had never been privileged to encounter such before – and perhaps, if he was given enough time and instruction to develop the requisite skills, he might eventually turn into such a man himself. That would really be something worth aiming for, now that he gave the idea a little thought.

"Did you like that, then?" asked Allan smugly, crawling up beside him, his long legs tangling with Dennis's.

"You know I did, you … you shameless bloody tart; you've really got a talent for that sort of thing, haven't you? How in God's name did you ever learn to do it in the first place?"

"Started young and got a lot of practice," came the rueful response. "You're not the first man I've ever been with, in case you hadn't guessed by now. Not by quite a long way, in fact. I was a gentleman's son; I went to public school and then to Cambridge. It was absolutely delicious there in those days – you could get everything you ever wanted, as long as you were prepared pay for it. Which, of course, I was."

"Money well spent, then, if you're asking me." Dennis leaned down and kissed him, tasting himself alongside bathtub claret and tobacco in the depths of Allan's mouth. "You can do that to me again, any bloody time you like, and maybe one of these days you'll teach me the way of it as well."

"I'd be happy to," replied Allan, "if I thought there'd ever be a chance." He sank back then against Dennis's shoulder, and for a long while after that the two of them simply stayed as they were, staring at the shadowed ceiling, listening to the crump of falling mortars and the distant chatter of a Vickers machine-gun. "It all seems to be happening so far away from here," continued Allan, after a while, "but we'll have to go back to it eventually, you know. We've been lucky to have this little interlude, but I'm very much afraid it can't last beyond morning."

"You don't believe we'll ever be able to come back here, then?" Dennis was holding Allan close to him, stroking his hair affectionately, fingertips playing caressing games across his neck and shoulders.

"No, I'm sorry to say I think that's rather doubtful. In fact I was always quite certain this would be our one and only chance. You know as well as I do that we'll have to go back to the real world tomorrow."

"The real world? I'm not at all sure what that is any more, or even if it actually exists." Regardless of the intimate nature of the setting, Dennis was uncertain of the wisdom of admitting this; he had the ghastly misgiving that it might be used against him at some future date, and that was almost more a more frightening prospect than having their night-time activities exposed to ridicule.

Allan shook his head slowly. "I have an odd idea that there may actually be more than one 'real world'," he said carefully, as though testing the words to see if they made any kind of sense. "And just at the moment, you and I are stuck somewhere in between them. So when we get up and get dressed in the morning, we have no idea what might be waiting for us outside that door. Whatever it is, though, there will be duties that we both have to perform, and other people that we'll have to be responsible to and for, and that in turn means that we probably ought to get a little sleep while we've got the opportunity. Much as I hate to waste even a minute of our time together," he continued, yawning, "I'm afraid there's a limit to what I'm capable of tonight if I'm still going to be of any practical use tomorrow."

Which, although Dennis didn't say as much, made perfect but rather unwelcome sense to him. "All right, then. If you really think it's for the best."

"I do, I'm afraid. And if it's truly all over between us – as it probably must be, all things considered – well, you've given me more than enough, in a short few hours, to make certain I'll remember you – and this lovely night of ours – until my dying day."

And only an acerbic twist of laughter afterwards served to identify this sentiment as the blacker-than-the-blackest gallows humour that it so manifestly was.

11

The room was lighter when Dennis next awoke, and the sounds of the barrage had died away to nothing. One bird sang in the hostel garden, such a plaintive little tune that if anyone had ever wanted to set words to it they would have needed to be unbearably sad. It was a song of separation, if ever he'd heard one; winter was closing in upon them, and from now on the poor thing would always be alone.

At his side Allan was just beginning to stir, his head turning on the thin pillow; they had made a tragic mess of this bed with their efforts during the night, but had somehow managed to bring the rough woollen blankets up around themselves and cut out the worst of the chills and draughts, and had therefore been surprisingly warm. Or maybe it was proximity and the aftermath of a bout of vigorous exercise which had accounted for that.

Dennis extracted himself carefully, doing his best not to wake his companion, but all his efforts proved to have been fruitless when Allan shifted in the bed and spoke to him.

"Are you leaving?" he asked, raising himself up onto one elbow and fixing Dennis with what – even in the pre-dawn gloom – could have been described as an accusatory stare.

"I should do, shouldn't I?" Dennis asked him, frankly. "The longer I leave it, the more difficult it's going to be to sneak out of here unseen. The girl in the kitchen – Marguerite – starts work really early, doesn't she?"

"Well, maybe she'll be late today," suggested Allan, the note of pleading in his voice almost matching that of the lonely singer in the garden. "And maybe she wouldn't tell on you if she saw you, anyway; I've always had the notion she seemed like rather a good sport."

Dennis thought about that for a moment.

"Listen, if we got caught together it would be embarrassing for you, but it would almost certainly be a lot worse for me. You're an officer, you can always talk your way out of things – you can blame it on your nerves and get yourself sent away to a nice comfortable hospital somewhere to be cured – but you know bloody well that the same thing wouldn't happen to me, especially if the powers that be decided they were going to deal with it as mutiny or desertion … "

"I know, and I honestly do appreciate your point of view," said Allan, soothingly. "Although it's not as if either of us ever had a realistic chance of getting home in one piece anyway, is it? I'm afraid you and I have pretty much seen the last of 'England, home and beauty' for a while – at least for this campaign, anyway."

"I understand that," responded Dennis. "But what I'm really trying to say is this; if ever I do have to be shot at dawn, I'd very much prefer it to be by the enemy rather than our own side – that is, if you don't object too much!"

"Yes, of course," was the more subdued reply. "And I'm very sorry; I really should have thought of that myself."

A few minutes later, Allan was sitting up against the head rail of the bed with the pillow squashed behind him, smoking thoughtfully and watching as Dennis rinsed his face and hands in the water from the jug. He had half-contemplated a trip into the adjacent bathroom, but that had felt too much like courting discovery so he'd opted instead for making use of the traditional chamber pot under the bed, and washing himself in cold water before carefully sponging his uniform. By trench standards this was tantamount to luxury in any case, and although he would not have time to shave he would certainly be as presentable as a great many of his comrades. Whatever some of the stuffier and more regimented regular officers had to say on the subject – and it was all right for them, they had batmen and servants to help them to maintain their appearance! – in the front line it didn't much matter what a man looked like as long as he was able to do his job. Nevertheless Dennis had borrowed a comb and slicked his hair down with water, and was even now climbing carefully back into his uniform.

"You'll go out through the garden, I suppose, will you?" asked Allan. "I presume that was how you got in?"

"Safer than trying to get that front gate open," said Dennis. "You know how it squeaks, it'd wake up everybody in the street. No, I'll climb out over the roof of the potting-shed, drop down into the baker's yard, and go out that way."

"They'll be working in there this morning," Allan reminded him soberly.

"I know; I promise I'll be careful. With a bit of luck I should be able to get out as far as the street without anybody seeing me, and I shouldn't have too much trouble making my way back to my unit from there. As for you – well, you really ought to go back to sleep for a while, if you can possibly manage it."

But Allan was shaking his head. "Not a chance," he replied decisively. "I'll wait until after you've gone, then I'll sort everything out and pack up my belongings ready to leave. No point in hanging about, after all, is there?"

"I suppose not." Dennis was buttoning his tunic, smoothing it down, checking that he had everything he was supposed to have. "Do you reckon we'll ever see each other again, then?" he asked. "It would be a bloody shame if not."

Allan shrugged, crushing out his cigarette. "Then I suppose it may have to be a bloody shame," he allowed, "although anything's possible. It's hopeless to try to predict what might happen. I wish we could, though; I wish we could spend more time together – and perhaps not all of it in bed."

"I don't imagine we'd have much in common if it wasn't for that, do you?" said Dennis, his mouth twisting wryly. "What would the two of us ever find to talk about, for a start? We're from completely different worlds – well, different classes, at any rate."

"Perhaps," acknowledged Allan. "Although it would be nice to have the chance to find out. Now," he added, swarming up out of the bed, naked and pale in the bedroom's pre-dawn light, "I hope you're going to behave like a proper gentleman and kiss me goodbye? And I'm not just talking about a quick peck on the cheek, thank you very much; I trust you to make a better job of it than that."

"All right."

Dennis did his best to make this seem like grudging capitulation, but in reality he could think of very few things he'd rather do. They hadn't spoken much about affection – there hadn't really been time, and anyway it had felt out of place somehow – but for all the urgency of their encounter there had also been a degree of tenderness between them. Kissing this man, therefore, would present him with very little of a problem; it was not as if he'd never actually done it before.

Settling his hands on Allan's bare shoulders, he was surprised to discover how warm he was – or how cold he was himself – and pulled him closer, his hands sliding easily down to Allan's waist and further still, over skin that was smooth and silky and seemed to sing beneath his fingers.

"I could quite easily have you again right now," he confided, ardently.

"I'm sure you could, darling," came the all-too-knowing response, "and I could quite cheerfully let you, but perhaps we ought to save it for another time?"

And Dennis, startled by what appeared to have been a thoroughly misplaced endearment, could think of nothing better to do at the moment than to stop him speaking, to make this no more difficult than it must be already by closing his mouth in the most effective manner possible. Allan's lips beneath his were warm and yielding and Allan – tall by most standards but not quite Dennis's equal – was as quiescent in his arms as any swooning moving-picture heroine, and perhaps for the first time Dennis understood that this might not simply be about sex after all. He had never really considered that it had anything to do with romance, or possibly even with love, yet if this was indeed the case he could be walking away not merely from a casual acquaintance with whom he'd shared a night of pleasure, but from someone who could – had the circumstances been conducive – have turned out to be the love of his life.

In any event, it would be better not to think about it. Too great a consciousness of what he might be losing, and he would not be able to leave at all. That was the way they all learned to feel eventually, once they got up as far as the front line; they were fighting for the future of whatever they held most dear – family, country, freedom – but it did not do to clasp it too close to one's heart when there was a job of work to be done. In time, perhaps, the men who survived the war would return and take up the threads of their lives again, and then they would be able to enjoy all the benefits of their own and their comrades' sacrifices. For now, however, such delights as those which Allan represented were probably best to be kept firmly at arm's length and not thought of in any detail for a while.

"Another time," Dennis acknowledged, as he ended the kiss. "But I'm going to have to leave you now, I'm afraid; I've got work to do today, and so have you."

"Yes, of course – but I'll watch you from the window as you go, if you wouldn't mind."

"All right." And then, because there was nothing remotely the equivalent of 'goodbye' that Dennis could ever have said to this man with a clear conscience, or that would not have caused him to falter in his duty more than he had already, he said the only thing that he could think of that he could still mean with all his heart. "I'm sorry," he told Allan, more brusquely than he meant to, and left the room without even once succumbing to the temptation of looking back.

He was a dozen paces down the corridor before the quiet sound of the door closing had stopped reverberating in his mind, and the careful noise of his footsteps on the stairs down to the education room came almost as a surprise. All in all his progress had a dreamlike character, as though he was slowly becoming detached from reality; he lurched through the world as if drunkenly, trusting that he would not be seen but taking no great precautions to avoid it, feeling that if he could only pass the kitchen door and get out into the garden he would be safe from observation, and neither his own reputation nor Allan's would have to suffer at all. Not that there would be any inducements which could ever persuade him to admit where he had been, whom he had been with, or what he had been doing; it would be safer, as he had suggested to Allan, to pretend to be a thief – an excuse which wouldn't work very well, he realised belatedly, if he wasn't carrying something that would make it look as if climbing over a wall to enter somebody else's house had been a worthwhile exercise.

On the way through the hall, therefore, he picked up a silver cigarette lighter and a photograph in a silver frame from the sideboard. They were quite valuable for their small size and would fit easily into the pockets of his coat, and they would simply have to be enough. He could always abandon them in the baker's yard, where hopefully they would be found and returned to the hostel in due course. They wouldn't have been particularly rich pickings for any experienced burglar, but for a shiftless opportunist soldier like himself they would do very well indeed, and Dennis knew precisely how to play up the characterisation if ever he was called upon to answer questions. That was the process the music-hall conjurors called legerdemain, the art of concealing one action under cover of another, and men with the proclivities he and Allan shared were no doubt obliged by their very nature to do this all the time; to dissemble, to misdirect, to draw away suspicion and to place it very firmly elsewhere. Whatever might have been the benefits of pursuing a greater and more permanent involvement with Allan – assuming the circumstances had been at all disposed to allow of it – there would always still have been the over-riding necessity for concealment, for dissembling the truth of their connection, and he was well aware that a life which had to be lived out under such conditions would scarcely have been worthy of the name.

The hobnails in Dennis's boots scratched like the claws of a cat along the multi-coloured encaustic tiles in the kitchen passageway, and he was once again fearful of being overheard. By this time of the day there should surely be someone moving about; Marguerite, the maid who arrived early every morning to light the boiler and produce hot water for the officers' baths, take round their jugs of shaving water and cook breakfast, should have let herself in by now, and it would be almost impossible to leave through the back door and pass into the garden without her setting eyes on him. He still made every effort to conceal his progress, however, pressing close to one wall, moving as easily and lightly as any broad-shouldered man over six feet in height well may, scarcely aware of the sounds he was making and keeping his attention focussed on listening for the girl. She was a small creature, not much more than sixteen or seventeen years old, with huge, shining brown eyes and a tangled mass of golden Pre-Raphaelite hair, extremely attractive in a domestically feminine way; Dennis had never had very much conversation with her himself – his French and her English both being laughably inadequate – but he knew that there were a great many men on the Western Front, officers and other ranks both, who believed that she was one of the prettiest girls in Belgium and imagined themselves to be in love with her. Certainly whenever he'd encountered her she'd always seemed to have a pleasant disposition, usually downright cheerful, and those who'd convalesced at the hostel had been universally willing to swear that her agreeable nature had contributed to their recovery.

Nearing the kitchen, he could hear the industrious rattle of bucket and coal-shovel; someone was clearly firing the boiler, which was a very good thing as far as he was concerned. Apart from anything else, the position of the range in the kitchen meant that whoever was attending to it – and he had to assume that it was Marguerite – would have their back turned towards him as he passed, unless he was exceedingly unlucky. Nevertheless he took no chances, leaning heavily against the door-frame and taking a careful look into the room. Just as he had expected, however, Marguerite was on her knees feeding the mouth of the furnace, all her attention on that task and nothing to spare for him. Seizing the chance, therefore, he was across the doorway in one hasty movement, down the passage to the back door, and had managed to get it open and himself outside it and into the garden before he could completely register that Marguerite had not only been shovelling coal but that she had also been sobbing as powerfully as if her heart was breaking.

To his regret, Dennis could not allow himself to think about that now, self-preservation being his first priority as he stole cautiously down the gravel path under shelter of the wall. That didn't make him any the less sympathetic, however; Heaven knew there were reasons enough to cry in wartime – fear and loss being chief among them – and on the whole it was perhaps surprising that more people didn't break down and sob while they went about their everyday affairs. Or perhaps they did, and he had simply been too absorbed in his own concerns to realise it.

At the point where the pergola stood away from the wall, the line of the garden dog-legged away to the right. This was therefore the last point at which anyone walking along the path could expect to see a face in one of the hostel's windows, and here Dennis paused. He was half-reluctant to turn, in fact, fearing that there would be nobody looking back towards him; already the previous night had begun to retreat into the realm of myth and legend, and he would not have been entirely sure that any of it had happened at all, had it not been for a curious feeling of enervation and a tingling sensation still playing upon his lips. And yes, he could just about see a blurred face under a cap of shining pale hair, and a slim hand that lifted to him in farewell, and he could not help remembering the touch of both that hand and its companion here, there and everywhere about his person. They were not close enough for details to be visible but he was certain which expression would be showing on Allan's face, and he knew it was one of regret.

He remembered that look of old; that was the way Allan had looked at him out of the back of the ambulance; it had skewered through him then, and it did so now. It left him feeling isolated and incomplete, knowing he must go on but not sure how – or what it was he was going on towards. What was certain, however, was that he could not remain where he was. With a last jaunty wave of parting, therefore – trying to convey to Allan that this really was a most insignificant state of affairs, nothing to worry about, and they would be fools to concern themselves with it at all – he stepped around the angle of the garden and sought the place where the potting-shed roof gave access to the top of the high boundary wall. There it was possible for a man, if he had any degree of agility about him at all, to climb in and out of the premises undetected. One foot on the big wooden wheelbarrow, that was the way; one knee on the tar-papered roof of the shed, one hand on the brick coping along the summit of the wall, and then he was almost home and dry. His heart thudded fiercely from exertion and wheeling colours spun wildly through his head; his senses were teetering and his hands had unaccountably begun to lose their grip. Dennis struggled on, however, trying to pull his body where his hands had been, to lift himself clear of the garden, but there was air under his feet, the wheelbarrow had shifted, and then he knew he was falling. There was time enough only for his brain to register that he was surely going to be hurt by this, and even more surely that he was going to lose his dignity, before he slammed suddenly into the unyielding ground, the breath was knocked out of him, and he lost himself all at once in a cloud of dark forgetting.

12

After a short while Dennis shook himself, clambered awkwardly to his feet, brushed soil and gravel from his jeans and leather jacket, and reached into his pocket for his cigarettes and lighter. It was full daylight now, although the sun had risen into cloud and there was a cold breeze cutting viciously through the garden. He stepped away from the remains of the rotted old wooden wheelbarrow – it had somehow collapsed beneath him, he realised, although why he had been attempting to climb on it in the first place he couldn't quite remember. That would be concussion, then, probably; he'd had the same before a time or two, whether playing rugby or boxing at school, and he may or may not have fallen off a horse on one occasion. Or perhaps it had been a seaside donkey on the beach at Scarborough. In any event, it didn't feel particularly serious this time, although he wasn't sure if you could really judge that sort of thing from the inside. Someone else would have to tell him whether or not he was making any sense, that was all; someone else would have to ask him questions that would test the functioning of his brain. Concussed or not, it would be safest right now for him to go back into the house and be with other people for a while.

Which was a shame, really, because being with other people was something he didn't especially want to do at the moment.

Nevertheless, he'd retained enough common-sense to over-ride his own anti-social prejudices, which in itself probably indicated that he was not too badly injured. He would swallow a couple of headache tablets and attempt to force down a few mouthfuls of breakfast, and after that he should have received a clear indication of whether or not it would be safe for him to make any attempt to drive the van. If he couldn't, Gus would definitely not be thrilled – but that, Dennis thought, was safer than being driven by a man who might collapse at any moment, and he was therefore quite willing to hazard the likelihood of Gus's displeasure.

He stamped out his cigarette before he entered the back door, and as he did so his nostrils were filled with the welcome scent of grilling bacon. He'd just about had it with so-called continental breakfasts on this trip – a few squares of rubbery cheese, some unidentifiable cold meat and a dollop of thin blackcurrant conserve were not at all his idea of a decent meal, and if it hadn't been for the assorted products of Messrs. Kelloggs his breakfasts would have comprised almost entirely of coffee, cigarettes and an overwhelming sense of futility.

Madame Duclos was bustling about in the kitchen as usual, and seemed to be the only one stirring. However she looked so self-contained, and seemed so happy at her task, that Dennis made no attempt to speak to her. Instead he went up to his room to grab a couple of Aspirin and then wandered back down to the hall, which he had not been able to see at all clearly during the previous evening. Now, however, there was daylight coming in through the semi-circular window above the door and it fell directly onto the sideboard, the guest book, the pile of leaflets about the building's history and the candles which stood waiting for visitors who seldom, if ever, seemed to arrive. He could see why this place was considered suitable for housing over-stressed priests; once that front door was closed, the modern world scarcely seemed to exist any more, and an individual in search of peace and quiet would undoubtedly have been able to find it here.

Not this morning, though. Somewhere on the landing above him there was the sound of bad-tempered grunting and the inconsiderate slamming of a bedroom door, and someone declaring loudly that they could eat a fuckin' 'orse, and a moment later Brian and Gary were thundering down the stairs towards him.

"Mornin', Dennis!" exclaimed Gary, several hundred decibels too loud for Dennis's wilting spirits. Heaven save him from people who had the energy to be this bouncy in the mornings!

"Gary," he said, calmly. "I see you slept all right, then?"

Gary shrugged. "'s a lot easier, innit, when you're on you own? Bloody women take up half the bloody bed."

Dennis's brow creased at this. "I thought that was the point," he said, "when you share a bed? You have half and they have half?" Or, his subconscious reminded him, you end up with your back against the wall because you want them to be comfortable, and you really don't mind about that at all.

"Yeah, well, that's the trouble, isn't it? They want half of bloody everything, except maybe your soul – and, in my opinion, they want all of that."

"Well, aren't you a cheerful bugger?" returned Dennis. And the truth of it was, of course, that if he wanted common sense this morning he'd be far more likely to get it out of Brian than Gary. Brian had been a few steps behind his louder colleague, and was now rummaging through his pockets for something he had apparently mislaid.

"Lost my bloody lighter," he explained, grumpily. "It's probably up in the room somewhere; I'll have to have a proper look for it after breakfast. Is that bacon I can smell?"

"Of course it's bloody bacon. She's used to having English visitors, didn't she say? Well, that'll be the full English, then." Gary, who had not been the one addressed, had taken it upon himself to answer anyway. "All this and full English for a fiver a night each? Can't go wrong here, can you? She must be cutting her own throat with prices like that."

"I suppose so," acknowledged Brian. "Although I don't think she does a lot of business, so she's probably lost track of what everybody else is charging. Or maybe she just does it for the company – she does seem to live here on her own, after all."

That was true. Dennis hadn't really stopped to think about it before, but in the old days an establishment like this would have taken several people to run it – cooks, cleaners, gardeners, and someone else to hold it all together and deal with the paperwork. Now it seemed to be only one little old lady, cheerful and enthusiastic though she was, trying to manage everything. How did she even get up and down all those stairs, which could be quite a challenge for a healthy man? Who did the laundry, who carried the coal, who kept the garden neat and tidy? he wondered. Surely she could not literally do it all by herself?

"Is Greta coming down?" he asked, changing the subject before he could confuse himself utterly.

"No idea," shrugged Gary. "I knocked on her door last night when we got back from the bar, and she told me to bugger off."

"I'm not surprised," laughed Dennis. "She wanted her rest, didn't she, poor girl?"

"Well, I was only going to give her a goodnight kiss." Gary's tone was peevish with entitlement. "Wouldn't have done her any harm to let me in, would it?"

"It would have, if she was throwing up all night," countered Brian, with a grimace. "You should just have let her sleep, you selfish sod. As it happens," he added, in a quieter tone, "I bumped into her outside the bathroom a few minutes ago. She said she wouldn't be wanting anything to eat, but she might come down for a cup of coffee later on. She looked a bit green about the gills," he concluded, "but I think she's pulling herself together all right. Apparently she carries industrial-strength painkillers, but she's always a bit woozy the morning after."

"Yeah," laughed Gary, "like me. Only she doesn't have the fun of going out drinking the night before." They were making their way slowly down the corridor towards the kitchen, and long before they reached the doorway Allan and Gus had already managed to catch up with them.

"Morning!" Gus sounded rested and cheerful, in sharp contrast to Allan who could barely manage a mumbled greeting and made no attempt to look in Dennis's direction at all. "Let the dog see the rabbit, eh? I'm ready for my breakfast today and no mistake." And with these words, and an enthusiastic chafing of the palms of his hands, he elbowed through the little group in the doorway and preceded them into the kitchen.

Madame Duclos evinced nothing but delight to see them all this morning, and – after a few polite enquiries as to how well they had slept and the state of Greta's health – she set to with a will and served up breakfast for the five of them, everything of the highest quality and more than enough of it to go around. Dennis, finding himself at the head of the scrubbed-pine table, was in an ideal position to look around and take in his surroundings rather more comprehensively than he had been able to manage the night before, when they had all been in a state of near-exhaustion and would cheerfully have slept on rusty barbed-wire if it had turned out to be necessary. He hadn't thought it through before, but no electricity presumably meant no refrigerator or freezer, no mixers or blenders or choppers in the kitchen, no tumble-dryer – and heating and cooking every single thing with coal. This only made sense if Madame had an army of little elves who came in to help her every day, and vanished again unseen; perhaps there were numerous sons and daughters and an ever-expanding tribe of grandchildren and great-grandchildren that she could call on for assistance in a crisis.

"Have you got children, Madame?" he asked her, as she replenished his coffee cup, and then he wished he hadn't. The kindly light went out of her eyes, and she stood regarding him almost sorrowfully whilst she formulated a careful answer.

"I had two sons," she said. "*Morts dans la guerre.*"

"The war?" Dennis's head was so full of Wipers, Whitesheets and the Vimy Ridge that for a moment he struggled to make sense of what she was telling him. "Oh, wait, you mean the other one? The Second … ?"

"*La deuxième guerre mondiale?*" put in Allan gruffly, helping him out. Half-guiltily Dennis glanced in his direction to thank him, but Allan had looked away already.

"One in the *FNFL* at the Battle of Dakar, the other in the *Commandos de Marine* on D-Day, still only boys. Their father was Duclos, the baker."

"The baker? Oh, you mean from the bakery next door?" Dennis pointed to the wall between the houses.

"Yes. In those days, that was his family's business; now – well, *ça appartient à des autres.*"

"Other people. Of course." And that was it, apparently; only two sons, and both killed, no bright daughters-in-law, no sturdy grandsons, no toddling great-grand-children wiping their jam-sticky hands all over the furniture. She was alone with her memories in her neat-as-a-pin house, except for the occasional ailing Catholic priest or the even more occasional stranded English visitor. No wonder she had been willing to make such a fuss of them.

"*On fait ce qu'on doit,*" the old lady told him quietly, and Dennis didn't really need Gus's low-voiced translation to make sense of it,

because her meaning had been clear enough. *We do what we have to do.*
That could have been the story of his life.

Angus and Gary went out in the garden for a smoke after breakfast, and Brian disappeared back upstairs with the avowed aim of searching for his lighter. Dennis followed him, but it did not take long to put his meagre belongings in order and lug his travelling bag back down the stairs. Heaven knew he wasn't the world's most meticulous man when it came to clothing and personal appearance, but even he would be glad to see the back of these jeans and this pair of boots for a little while, and to have an unlimited choice of clean underpants and tee-shirts at his disposal. Not that they weren't all in much the same boat, come to think of it, although women always seemed better prepared for this sort of thing than men.

Dumping his bag in the hall while he waited for the others he found his eyes drawn to a photograph of the young man in a silver frame, so carefully placed that it was certain to be one of the landlady's most cherished possessions. The subject looked somehow slightly familiar, although Dennis couldn't immediately place him; young and cheerful and with a pipe stuck in the corner of his mouth, he wore the uniform of the Royal Flying Corps as if it was a set of cricket flannels, utterly relaxed and clearly in the market for a challenge – one of those privileged young men who for a while had found the experience of war to be tremendous fun. If he could have spoken, the first words out of his mouth would undoubtedly have been, "What the hell are we waiting for, old boy? Why don't we just get on out there and do something, eh?"

One thing was for sure, though; this could not possibly be Duclos, because – and admittedly Dennis's knowledge of the subject was limited to a TV series he remembered watching more than a decade earlier – he didn't imagine there had been too many provincial French bakers in the Royal Flying Corps. In fact he seemed to recollect that the pilots had all been upper-class public school types, and anyone from a less advantageous background had been confined to a ground crew role. So who could this dashing young adventurer be, then, and why had Madame taken such great care with the placement of his portrait – in a position of eminence just below the crucifix on the wall?

"This is a picture of the Honourable Bryant," supplied Madame softly, coming up behind him. He hadn't heard her approach at all, so absorbed in speculation had he been. "*Il avait vingt ans quand il est mort.*"

"*Vingt ans*. Twenty years old when he died."

"Twenty."

"Was he your boyfriend?" And just where that question had come from, Dennis could not rightly have explained, even to himself.

"Oh, well ... " For a moment Madame fluttered and seemed embarrassed, her chalky cheek taking on the very slight hint of a richer colour. "But his parents were *bourgeois* and mine were peasants. We would never have been allowed to marry, and in any case I was too young."

"Sixteen, seventeen?" he speculated idly.

"Seventeen, yes."

"But he died anyway, and so you married the baker."

"As you say," nodded Madame, slowly. "But that was not until later – and he was older and had sons already. Well, they are all dead now, too."

So he had been right about her; she was a survivor, one of those immensely strong but pitiable women who had watched her loved ones die off one by one and yet had somehow found a way to keep going herself.

"We do what we must?" asked Dennis, repeating her earlier words back to her. It all sounded horribly bleak to him, to have enjoyed a short and delightful flirtation with the Honourable Bryant, whoever he might have been, and then to have settled down to life with the baker Duclos; to have briefly had the best, and then forever afterwards to have made do with whatever was left behind. If that wasn't an object lesson in seizing one's happiness whenever it came along, because there might never be another chance, than he did not know what it was.

Madame, however, had shuffled off back towards the kitchen again, and although he turned to speak to her he could not quite bring himself to intrude upon her mood of reflection. He was still staring at the portrait therefore, without a brain in his head, when Brian came clattering back down the stairs a short while later and deposited his weekend bag next to Dennis's in the hallway.

"Found it!" he exclaimed triumphantly. "My lighter," he added, when Dennis turned a bewildered gaze towards him.

"Oh yes, right. Good."

"What you got there, then?" Brian peered over his shoulder, squinted at the picture, and pursed his lips. "Looks a little bit like my dad," he said, thoughtfully. "Can't be him, though; he wasn't born 'til some time after the First World War – and anyway he was in the Tank Corps in North Africa. Could be another relative, though, maybe."

Dennis had never met Brian's dad, but he didn't have the slightest hesitation in acknowledging the family resemblance; seeing them together like that, virtually side by side, had made him realise why the photograph had seemed so familiar to him in the first place. The likeness to some relative of Brian's father was unquestionable to his way of thinking; apart from a few minor details, like the hair and the pipe and the uniform, the picture of the individual in the silver frame could very well have been a younger portrait of Brian himself.

13

Within half an hour they had all assembled. Greta, still looking pale and decidedly wobbly, slipped out of the house with Dennis when he went to unlock the minibus, and established herself in her seat with her blanket and a handful of tissues while he went into the store to buy her a bottle of Evian. By the time he returned the others had made their way back to the cobbled market square, carrying their belongings, and disposed themselves in various places around the bus.

"Nice old girl, wasn't she?" asked Gary, as he clambered in. "Very friendly. Very sorry to see us go. Even gave Angus a big hug and told him to be careful – I expect she thought he'd probably be doing the driving."

Dennis could not help raising an eyebrow at this, and when he looked up it was to find to his surprise that Allan was looking back at him, a composed but thoughtful expression on his face. He was biting his lower lip nervously, however.

"All right, mate?" Dennis asked him, quietly.

"I suppose so. I must admit I didn't really want to leave the place at all; there's just something about it – the garden, in particular. It's just so … " He shrugged, clearly not finding the expression he had wanted to use.

"Tranquil?" Dennis was glad Gary couldn't hear him; any word that suggested a wider vocabulary than was necessary for discussing birds, booze and football was automatically anathema to Gary, and likely to bring forth a cry of "Coo, aren't we posh!" and "Oo swallowed the dictionary, then?" It did seem, on the other hand, to have struck a chord with Allan, and there was a distinct look of gratitude in his eyes.

"Tranquil," he repeated, nodding. "She's very lucky to live there all the time; I'd give my right eye just to have the chance."

"Yeah, me too. But I'm not sure if 'lucky' is the word I'd use." Dennis was on the point of saying more, and then it came to him that perhaps it wouldn't be the most charitable thing in the world to pass on the details of Madame Duclos's story, especially as she'd told him in such a confidential manner. He'd had the clear impression that her words had been meant for him alone – and that, combined with the picture of the man who wasn't Brian – had served to make him extra cautious. "So, you're navigating for me this morning, are you?"

"I'm afraid so. It should be simple enough, shouldn't it? Back the way we came, to the junction near the graveyard, and then out onto the other road, turn left, and no stopping after that until we get to Dunkirk."

"No stopping? I take it you're not up for a scenic tour of the battlefields of the First World War, then, are you?"

"No, I'm not. In fact, if I never see another bloody battlefield again it'll be too soon," said Allan, with emphatic vehemence.

Retracing their route of the night before, they were soon out of the village and onto a straight stretch of road that ran between tracts of featureless countryside so flat that the mild ridge that held the little white graveyard with its gleaming Cross of Sacrifice was visible a long time before they drew anywhere near it. Allan had been growing more and more pensive as they approached, glancing around fearfully at the empty countryside as though expecting to be on the receiving end of some kind of armed assault, and when eventually they reached the junction where they had turned off the previous evening Dennis paused the bus there for a long time while he considered what was best to do.

"We really don't have a choice about this, do we?" he said quietly to Allan.

"No," came the agitated response, the tone too low for the others in the back to overhear. "I don't think we do, I'm sorry to say."

That was all Dennis needed. He put the van into gear again, pulled away and brought the wheel hard around to the right.

"'Ere, 'ang on!" shouted Gary. "You're going the wrong way!"

"No we're not," Dennis told him, through gritted teeth. "This is the right way; I'm afraid you're going to have to trust us for the time being."

There was a little pull-out place just off the road, which Dennis had failed to notice the evening before, but which must have been where Gus had pulled the minibus off the road to wait for them; it was a strip of crushed limestone just large enough to take a couple of vehicles. Dennis parked there now, took the keys out of the ignition, and got out of his seat.

"Well," he said, "this is it." His eyes lifted to the horizon line, to a small grove of trees some distance away across the field on the far side of the road. He could hear Gary saying something loaded with profanity and Brian telling him to shut his fuckin' mouth or Brian would shut it for him, and then he became acutely aware of Allan standing quietly by his side. "This is bloody it, isn't it?"

"Yes," said Allan, and he was shivering.

"Oh well, in for a penny." Dennis strode forward, pushed open the gate, and held it for Allan to go through. "Let's go in and get it over with, then, shall we?"

Within the shelter of the low, white wall the turf was a close-cropped emerald carpet into which were set a number of matching white headstones. Travelling in this part of northern Europe such things had become a familiar sight, but even so the majority of travellers would simply have gone on past – unless they had been here specifically for the purpose of visiting one or other of these manicured enclaves. Dennis had heard Belgium described as 'the cockpit of Europe' – an expression which had caused ribald laughter in his history class at school, simply because their usually very proper teacher had actually uttered the word 'cock'. He'd managed to explain, through a barrage of ill-suppressed giggling, that there had been so many battles here, it had been fought over so many times, that nearly every spadeful of soil that was dug from the fields contained a memento of one or other of them – whether it was Oodenarde, Waterloo, Torville Wood, or the Battle of the Bulge. Only the more recent of these, however, had generated this endless series of enclosures – some vast, with massive central memorials covered in hundreds of thousands of names, and some like this one, with their small contingent of fallen commemorating just one action, perhaps only a single day, when the war had briefly been here and had then moved on, leaving only these behind.

"What do you suppose we'll find?" asked Allan, taking a few tentative steps along a mown strip between the graves. "Do we even know what we're looking for?"

Dennis shrugged. "We'll know it when we see it, I reckon," he said. At the moment it was all he could not to reach out and offer to take Allan by the hand; all the boundaries between them seemed to have fallen away, although he could not begin to understand the mechanism by which this had happened or what any of it might signify for himself or his future life. Nothing in his mind made very much sense at the moment anyway, from the football match to this morning's fall in the garden; he – or someone who looked like him, and who spoke in his voice – had spent the night with someone who might or might not have been Allan, and those two men had certainly enjoyed themselves – and each other – very thoroughly. Morning had brought a different kind of reality, however, and now they were tiptoeing together through a graveyard in the hopes of finding something neither of them had ever acquired the terminology to describe.

In the corner of the cemetery most distant from the road there was a sheltered place where a sweet chestnut tree was leaning over the wall. It looked as if it had been there much longer than either the graves or the wall itself, and had witnessed a great many of the wars Dennis's teacher had attempted to describe. Indeed its roots probably went under and through the whole calm square of earth, which must have made life a little difficult when these graves were originally being dug – but then, of course, it would have been a smaller tree in those days. At any rate it offered a natural focal point towards which – and without consultation – Dennis and Allan found their footsteps inevitably turning.

"Nice place to end up," said Allan, softly. "I wouldn't mind being here, or somewhere quite like it."

"No," conceded Dennis, "me neither."

"This would've been the casualty clearing station, I suppose. I read somewhere that a lot of the smaller cemeteries were just set up wherever people happened to be at the time. Of course, some of them were blown up again afterwards when the war moved back in the other direction, which is why there are so many men unaccounted for; it's not simply that they were unrecognisable when they were found. That's why you get things like this," Allan added, idly indicating a stone bearing the enigmatic inscription *A Sergeant of the Royal Engineers, Killed in Action, 21 October, 1916; Known Unto God.* "On the other hand, they may just not have found enough of him to identify."

Dennis shrugged. "Well, that wouldn't have mattered to him, would it? I mean, 'Known Unto God' is enough if you happen to believe in that sort of thing, and if you don't it's irrelevant anyway. Having a known grave is only important for the relatives, if they want to come over and visit and lay flowers or something."

"True. And this lot would probably all have known each other, anyway, so at least he's among his mates."

"Well, if they didn't know each other before, they've had plenty of time to get acquainted since," said Dennis. "I don't know, I've never worked out whether I believe in life after death or not; you can't really seem to have it without believing in God as well, and I've always had a bit of trouble with that. But I'd like to think something goes on living after the body dies."

"*Music, when soft voices die,*
Vibrates in the memory;
Odours, when sweet violets sicken,
Live within the sense they quicken.

Rose leaves, when the rose is dead,
Are heaped for the beloved's bed;
And so thy thoughts when thou art gone,
Love itself shall slumber on.

That's Shelley again, of course." Allan shook his head slowly, trying to dissemble this sudden outburst of romanticism. "He knew a thing or two about grief, didn't he?"

Dennis turned to look at him. "You're into poetry, then, are you?" he asked, clumsily.

Allan shrugged. "A bit. Not the sort of thing you can generally talk about at work, though, is it? People are liable to get the wrong idea."

"Maybe. But you don't really talk about yourself at all."

"Not if I can help it, I don't," Allan admitted, sniffing. "There's nothing much to say, and nobody's all that interested anyway."

"I am," protested Dennis. "Well, I mean, I could be. Potentially. You can talk to me, if you like." Which, now that he thought about it, was precisely the opposite of what he would have said twenty-four hours earlier, when his main priority had been making sure he found himself in any place where Allan currently wasn't. "We could maybe have a drink together one night or something?"

"Maybe." But Allan didn't sound entirely convinced, and almost without concentrating on what he was doing – as it seemed to Dennis – he moved away, standing in front of the next marker, reading it aloud perhaps because it was better than continuing with their rather too personal conversation.

"*Captain Gerald H. de V. OGLESBY*
18th Bn. (Bridlington) East Yorks. Regiment
Killed in Action, 21 October, 1916 : Aged 30
Until the day break and the shadows flee away.

I like that last bit," he added, trying a little too hard to manufacture a smile. "I wouldn't mind too much having that on my gravestone, you know."

Dennis turned to look at him, one eyebrow climbing steeply. Was it even possible, he wondered, that Allan hadn't realised yet what was going on? Did you have to have a mind that wasn't fettered by the teachings of organised religion, perhaps, or did you just need to be willing to think further outside the box than people usually did? Or did you maybe have to experience it for yourself and then somehow process what had happened, like a tone-deaf person suddenly learning to appreciate music?

"I'm not quite sure how to break this to you, Allan," he began, cautiously, "but I've got an idea that maybe that's just what you did have."

The silence seemed to stretch on for a very long time after that. There was a cold wind whistling, the distant thrum of a tractor moving back and forth over a corrugated field, and the uncouth chatter of their fellow-travellers back at the van. There was music, too, jangly and incomprehensible, from the radio. Between the two in the corner of the cemetery, however, there was not a single word – just the slowly-falling realisations which seemed to settle around them and accumulate like gentle flakes of snow. One alone might forever have remained invisible, but where there were more of them – and when they all came together – they altered the character of the landscape entirely.

"Are you honestly trying to tell me," Allan began, hesitantly, at last, "that any of what I'm remembering could actually be real? The ... the shell-hole? The ambulance? The ... what happened in the night?" There was a trembling stillness about him, as if he was facing something he could not fully comprehend.

"All of it was," said Dennis. "In a way. Don't get me started about what's real and what isn't – that could take a whole lifetime to sort out – but I think you and I remember some of the same things, don't we?"

"Well, yes – but are they really memories, though? I thought it was all far more likely to have been a dream. Especially ... " Allan stopped in some agitation, coloured violently, and his eyes turned down towards his boots. "What precisely do you remember about last night, Dennis?" he asked, his voice a strangulated half-whisper. "Tell me the worst, for fuck's sake."

Well, that wouldn't be too difficult. The fuzzy-headedness from the fall had gone completely now, and Dennis had retained a clear enough memory of how he'd passed the nocturnal hours. Clear, that was, except for the part around the edges, where he himself had stepped into and out of the picture.

"You and me," he said, as neutrally as he could. "We drank red wine, and then we ... well, do the words 'macassar oil' hold any significance for you?"

Allan seemed almost to crumple under the weight of the revelation. "Yes," he said, shakily. "They do. Oh, fuck, you won't tell anybody, will you? I haven't even ... I mean, not even my ex-wife ... well, not until the day she came home unexpectedly one day and found me watching a gay porn video – and then it all came out, of course ... " It seemed as if he was on the point of breaking down entirely then, and without a moment's hesitation Dennis slung a comradely arm around his shoulder and pulled him in for a brisk hug.

"I think you may have missed the part where the two of us were in it together," he said, wondering whether or not he should feel embarrassed about it. "Which isn't very flattering. I think we both enjoyed it, didn't we?"

"Well ... all right, thank you." Allan shrugged himself free from Dennis's arm, but still remained close beside him. "So," he asked, "the question is, was it actually us who did all that? Or was it them?" He gestured to the headstones in front of which they were standing. "You were in the Royal Engineers, weren't you, I seem to remember? Or he was, at any rate."

"I was," said Dennis, calmly accepting the identification, "but does it have to be either-or?" He was only processing the thought at the same time as he heard himself speaking the words, and hadn't got the first clue where he was going with it, but he didn't let that stop him. "Couldn't it have been us and them as well, somehow ... you know, at the same time?"

"I don't know, could it? How would that even work?" Allan sounded more than a little exasperated; this was clearly an intellectual challenge too far, where he was concerned.

"God knows!" The irony of this exclamation from a card-carrying atheist like himself was not entirely lost on Dennis. "But sometimes it isn't important to understand how a thing works, just as long as it goes on working. Isn't that actually the definition of faith?"

"This from an engineer," laughed Allan, starting to sound a little more relaxed and almost beginning to resemble his normal self. "I'd have thought verifiable facts would mean more to someone like you."

"Okay, you can laugh ... but if you'd seen half the rotten old machinery I've seen, being held together by rust and baling-twine and only keeping going out of habit, you'd know that it isn't just the components that're important; there has to be something else in the mix as well. Like willpower, maybe – or just plain bloody-mindedness?"

"So what you're saying is, there has to be an afterlife because some people are just too stubborn to accept that there isn't one? It's an attractive theory."

"It's that all right," conceded Dennis, smiling back at him. "And it's all because the world is full of stubborn sods like me who've never learned to take 'no' for an answer, and who probably never will."

14

"Did I ever actually know who you were?" Allan asked him, as they walked.

They had moved away from their corner and were now pacing slowly along the aisle between two rows of stones, more concerned with their inner selves than with anything that might be happening in the outside world. Dennis noticed, however, with a faint sense of bemusement, that Angus was outside the bus smoking, Gary had hopped over the drainage ditch and was loping across the opposite field towards the trees, and that Brian and Greta had remained in their seats but were apparently deep in conversation.

"I don't know. If you're asking me for a name, I haven't got one to give you, I'm afraid – but then you didn't remember what's-his-name Oglesby, either, did you? Well, I have no more idea than you did who I was back then. Oh, there might be a few stray memories," he added, trying his hardest to call them to mind, "but they're not at all clear – as if that tape's been played too many times and it's started to wear thin."

"Yes, I'm the same. Stuff you shouldn't know about because it wasn't you, but it's there in the background anyway. Troop ships and ammunition trains, cavalry horses, gun emplacements; people you met and people who died."

"People like us," said Dennis. "We died, didn't we? Both of us. We died on the same bloody day."

Allan didn't answer that immediately. When he did, though, he said, "Of course, there was only that one day."

"Aye, you're right there." Dennis fell silent again, for what felt like an age, and then he coughed awkwardly and the words began to fall out of him all in a bunch, tumbling over one another, because there was really no way of introducing this subject that would not be appallingly uncomfortable for both of them. "There's no nice way of saying this," he began, making little effort to conceal his distress, "but I reckon I might have seen you die. The ambulance took a direct hit, didn't it? It must have been quick – you and the other blokes in the back, you would all have gone more or less at once. I was standing on the road and I saw it happen, but there wasn't a bloody thing I could have done to stop it."

"Quick?" Allan was shaking his head in denial. "It was nothing like bloody quick enough, if you ask me. Did you seriously think I wasn't aware of what was going on, Dennis? I could see you too, you know; there was a window in the door of the ambulance, and I was looking out of it the whole time. Something came down from the sky and it fell directly on top of you – and you just went up like a Roman bloody candle, right there in middle of the road. I don't think you ever even tried to move away, or save yourself, or anything like that; you just stayed standing where you were – and that was how you died, still on your feet."

"Oh. So that's why I can't remember anything that happened afterwards."

"That would probably be the reason, yes."

The wholly surreal nature of the conversation was just something else that they would have to take in their stride, Dennis realised. The rational, sceptical part of his brain should have been questioning a great deal more about this than ever it had, but there was also a long-denied romantic in him which, on first encountering something that it didn't understand, was only too inclined to accept it at face value. In either case the result seemed to have been to bring him to Allan, whom he hadn't even known he wanted.

"So, we're ... what? Ghosts? Reincarnations or something?"

But Allan seemed to have no better handle on the situation than he had himself. "I can't even give you an educated guess," he admitted, dully. "I do know that I never had any strange past memories before we came here, though, so maybe it's something to do with the place? Could it just be because we're walking over the same bit of countryside, do you think? Or are there ... I don't know ... free-floating memories that latch onto any suitable candidate in the vicinity? Have ... your friend and mine ... " he indicated the two gravestones " ... done this over and over again, every time two men with the right sort of inclinations happened to drive past? Is Belgium full of dead men with unfinished business, constantly on the look-out for someone to stand in for them? Why am I even asking all these stupid questions – and why am I asking you, of all the bloody people in the world?" Exasperatedly, Allan ran a hand back through his hair. "I'm sorry, Dennis, I just feel as if I've taken something peculiar and my brain's been totally scrambled. There have been parts of this whole thing that actually felt quite straightforward at the time, and other parts that have totally confused the hell out of me – and I'm really getting to the point now where I wish it was all over, frankly."

"Yes." It wasn't until Allan had articulated the sentiment that Dennis became fully aware of just how much he'd been wishing that himself. "But look, if you're right – and I wouldn't be surprised if you were – then when we get back into the van and drive away from here we're probably going to lose any chance we might have had of figuring this out once and for all, and I'm a bit reluctant to let that go without making one last attempt to wrap my brain around it. After all, who knows what the hell's going to happen to us a couple of miles down the road; we're probably going to go back to not being able to stand one another, aren't we? So maybe we owe it to ourselves, and to them, to – I don't know, 'stay in their moment' just a little bit longer?" He produced the last words almost apologetically, aware of the note of pleading in his tone. It was absurd to be so reluctant to give up something that didn't really exist, and that probably wasn't at all important if it did, but when he thought about all the things he didn't have in his life and had never really imagined he stood a chance of acquiring, well, even the illusion of a temporary happiness with Allan – despite the emotional conflicts it produced within him – wasn't something he was willing to surrender without a fight.

"Well, I wouldn't want to keep the others waiting," Allan told him, with a wry attempt at a smile, "but since Gary seems to have taken up field-walking we won't really be holding anybody up if we stay where we are until he gets back. Besides, I actually feel quite comfortable here – and I even feel quite comfortable with you, and that's not something I ever thought I'd hear myself saying."

"Good." And Dennis was grinning at him then, wondering whether this was all over yet or not, and beginning to suspect that there might be more of the story still to be told. "Look, I don't want to confuse the issue, but ... did you ever have a proper look at that picture the old lady kept in the hallway at the hostel? The one in the silver frame?"

"The one that looked a little bit like Brian? Yes, I noticed that, too."

"Good. Only ... you remember telling me that you thought the body in the shell-hole might be Gary? Well, if he could be in two different places at once ... or in two different times at once, perhaps that's what I mean ... and you and I could, as it seems, then do you reckon maybe Brian could as well? Only, that chap in the picture was her boyfriend, and apparently his name was the Honourable Bryant and he died in the war, too – and if I'm right, then maybe he ought to be around here somewhere." An expansive hand-gesture took in the tidy enclosure with its small, exclusive complement of permanent residents; it was beginning to feel more and more like a privilege to have been selected to receive the particular distinction of burial here, and that in turn was making Dennis excessively curious about the other men with whom they had found themselves in company. "How about we split up and look for him?" he suggested, trying not to notice the incongruity of the proposal.

"Don't need to," said Allan. "He's right here, look:

Second Lieutenant
Hon. Charles R. BRYANT
Royal Flying Corps
23 January 1916: Aged 22
The Earth holds not a braver gentleman

That'll be him, won't it?"

"Yes, yes, it will." Dennis moved closer to it, and found himself blinking back a few tears at the sight, even though he was certain that he'd never known the man in life. "No wonder she was crying about him that morning."

"What's that?"

Dennis lifted his head sharply and stared at Allan, not quite realising what he had said until he heard the other man's response to it. "Well, the girl in the kitchen ... Marguerite; that morning when I left you ... uh, this morning, I suppose I mean ... " It was all just too complicated to parse, and for a moment or two he stopped short, mental gears slipping and sliding against one another in confusion; then he shook his head violently as if to clear it, and managed somehow to carry on speaking. "When I went out past the kitchen she had her back to me and she was crying. Madame Duclos told me that she and this Honourable Bryant bloke had wanted to get married at one time, but then he was killed and she married someone else, and I just ... I suppose because she was always in the kitchen, really, but ... well, I just put two and two together somehow and she's Marguerite, isn't she, and that's why she's still in the house?" The last part of this argument came out all in a rush, as though Dennis really wanted to give speech to the words before he could run out of courage altogether.

"Marguerite?" Allan was clearly delving into some half-forgotten reservoir of memory. "Yes, I can quite see that; Marguerite and Madame Duclos are the same person and we actually realised it, didn't we? Which is how we found our way to the hostel in the first place, of course. I knew it couldn't be just an accident; I knew it had to be something more than that."

"So Gary was the body in the pit, and you and I were those two guys in the corner over there, and Brian was this man, and that leaves ... No, no, it doesn't leave Angus at all, does it? Wasn't that who you were talking to in the education room last night, when you were trying to sneak me upstairs? The chap who was reading the Bairnsfather book?"

"The Padre?"

"Yes, the Padre. You were standing a lot closer to him than I was, weren't you? Well, what do you think?"

Allan chewed his lower lip a moment before replying. Then he said, quietly, "He was older than either of us, of course, but then so is Gus. I wouldn't have said they were identical, by any means, but there were definitely quite a lot of similarities. Yes, I think that identification would probably work for me. In which case, of course ... "

"Let's split up," suggested Dennis again. "We can do more damage that way."

Allan regarded him from a very short distance, with a cynically raised eyebrow and an expression of painful tolerance. "Are you really sure this is the appropriate time and place to be using a *Ghostbusters* reference?"

he asked, wryly.

"Actually, no," replied Dennis. "But the fact that you recognised it makes me wonder if we don't have quite a bit more in common than we thought."

It didn't take them long to trawl through the inscriptions on the rest of the markers and, by the time they had checked them all, Dennis and Allan found themselves once again in the sheltered corner where the boughs of the sweet chestnut leaned over from the field next door. One stone there had been slightly obscured and its colour subtly altered by generations of dropping leaves, but when they stood directly in front of it they had very little difficulty in making sense of the inscription.

Rev. Augustus ELGIN
Chaplain to the Forces
4th Class
18th April 1917: Aged 39
They die not, who live in the hearts
of those they leave behind.

"I would say that was fairly conclusive evidence, wouldn't you?" asked Dennis, for want of something to fill the uncomprehending silence.

At his side, Allan was nodding vigorously. "And look," he said, "have you noticed something else? Everywhere else in the graveyard the gap between the stones is exactly the same. Look." He turned round, and pushed his hand between two adjacent markers. "What's that, about four or five inches apart?" The next gap he measured was the same, and so was the next, and all the rest looked as if they would fit into the identical template, a regulation distance apart. "Over there, though ... "

He didn't need to add more. The two graves in which they were most particularly interested, those of Captain Oglesby and his unknown Sergeant of Engineers, were the merest fraction closer together than any of the others in the same enclosure.

"What d'you reckon that's all about?" continued Allan, his tone more mystified than troubled. "There's got to be a reason for it, surely?"

Dennis, in a spirit of co-operation, struggled to come up with some sort of rationale for the unusual adjacency. "Well, it could just be the roots of the tree," he speculated idly, "or something to do with the footings of the wall perhaps, but it's all much of a muchness, isn't it? Things just are, here, that shouldn't be – and that wouldn't be if we were anywhere else – and it doesn't really seem to be a lot of use wondering why or how they came about. Maybe what we should really be asking ourselves is what we're going to do about them – if anything – after we leave here. Which," he added, "we're going to have to do in a minute or two, by the looks of things, because here comes Gary – and what the hell is that he's carrying in his hand, the dipstick? He ought to know better than to pick up just any old odds and sods he bumps into in the fields round here!"

In a few more paces they had reached the gate and were out through it, back onto the side of the road. Gus was there already, and greeted the pair of them as they drew closer to him.

"All right now, lads? Problem solved, is it, whatever it was? Only we're running out of time if we're going to get to Dunkirk to get aboard this hypothetical ferry – which, frankly, I'll only believe in when I can see it."

"Yes, thanks, mate, we're fine." Because of course Gus knew – well, something, at least, but it was not a conversation Dennis could ever really imagine them having, somehow. Not without a good few drinks inside them, anyway, and maybe when the surface memories of this trip had faded away a bit and they could get the whole thing into some semblance of perspective.

"Oh aye," said Gus, comfortably. "I knew you would be, sooner or later. But what the hell this eedjit's playing about at, mind you, I wouldn't have a clue."

The three of them stood together in a group and watched Gary as he came belting down the narrow track at the edge of the opposite field and launched himself back over the drainage ditch like a Grand National horse negotiating the Water Jump, trotting up to them at last with an unbearably smug expression on his round, moonlike face.

"You total pair of tossers," he said, without malice, as he approached. He was slightly out of breath, but still capable of making himself understood. "There wasn't any bloody information board up there anywhere; you were telling total bloody porkies all along, the pair of you."

Dennis, prepared to stand his corner and feign the most absolute innocence until the cows came home, quirked an ironic eyebrow in Allan's direction before replying. "I'm not sure I like the tone of your voice, young man," he said to Gary, more amiably than he felt. "There's a perfectly good signboard up there, covered in all sorts of useful information about the Battle of Torville Wood, and if you couldn't see it then I think I'd be a bit worried about my eyesight if I were you."

"Or perhaps," put in Allan, in a clear but uncharacteristic attempt to be loyal and supportive, "that wasn't the same clump of trees that we were in last night. After all, it was dark, and foggy, and we didn't really know our way around."

"Oh, yeah, right," returned Gary, in a frankly disbelieving tone of voice. "And if that's the case, then I've got a bloody bridge I'd like to sell you. Look here, I have no idea what you two are up to and why you wanted to go haring off up there at the dead of night – it's a bloody long way for a Jimmy Riddle, and why the pair of you might've wanted to go off and do that together is something I'd rather not speculate about, to be honest – but that clump of trees, board or no board, is definitely the one you were in, and this is how I know it."

With which, and the addition of a stage magician's flourish and cry of 'ta-da!', he produced an object from inside his jacket and laid it across Dennis's open palm. Superficially it bore a horrifying resemblance to a German Model 24 stick grenade, but after only a single heartbeat of panic Dennis realised that it was in fact no such thing, although it had clearly been in the ground for a great many years and was covered in mud and in a fairly dilapidated and disintegrating state.

"Recognise it?" crowed Gary, as loud and aggravating as he had ever been, but this time also with the irrefutable certainty that for once in his life he was actually right. And Dennis, reluctant though he was, was obliged to concede the victory to him just this once.

"Of course I do," he answered, making a superhuman effort not to sound impressed. "This is the torch I borrowed from Brian."

15

For the next half-hour at least, Gary just could not shut up about the torch. They had changed places in the minibus, with Brian taking Allan's place in the front passenger seat and seeming totally focussed on the task ahead – getting them all safely aboard the ferry and on their way home to England. The crossing into France was accomplished without difficulty, and shortly after that they were on the main A25, where signboards with little white stencilled boats on them indicated that they were travelling in the right direction. Brian was virtually monosyllabic during this part of the journey – indeed, Gary was doing enough talking for all of them – and he only turned round once to say, "Fuck's sake, Gaz, it's only a bloody torch and it's mine anyway; if I don't care what happened to it then why the fuck should you?" which effectively silenced the flood of inanity for a while.

Traffic increased as they drew closer to the port, and Dennis's attention was naturally occupied with navigating safely through it. Brian's occasional instructions were not entirely necessary, on the whole, but he was glad to have them anyway, and the preoccupied silence which filled the rear compartment was also very welcome. On the run-in to the ferry terminal itself he found that he was leaning forward over the wheel, hyper-alert, his stress levels rising exponentially; then – out of nowhere, as it seemed – he heard Allan exchanging a quiet remark with Greta, and suddenly he felt a great deal more comfortable about everything. There was no denying that, whatever the feeling might be, it had seemed to diminish considerably as they drove further away from the graveyard, and at first he had experienced that with a sensation of relief, but there had also been regret that perhaps something was passing from his grip which on mature reflection he might have preferred not to lose. The simple fact was, however, that he had never had time for mature reflection in all this; all he had ever been able to do was react in the moment, and stand by the choices he had made.

Or maybe those choices had been made for him, although how or by whom he did not much care to speculate.

In a windy corner of the ferry terminal Dennis drew the minibus to a halt on Brian's instructions, and they all disembarked swiftly. The car park was half-full of British-registered vehicles, with a makeshift sign directing Turbo Ferries passengers to a Portakabin tacked onto a line of low-slung buildings slowly making their way out to sea. It was bleak there, and icy cold, and a van with a drop-down hatch was doing a roaring trade in tea and hot snacks.

"The Brits abroad," said Brian, shrugging apologetically. "A cup of tea, a ciggie and a bloody good moan; that's really all we ever need."

"Can't beat it," opined Gary, irrepressibly. He was already striding off to take his place in the queue for refreshments, leaving Greta – as weak-legged as any new-born calf – standing irresolutely behind with the others.

"All right, luv?" Brian asked her, solicitously.

"I will be," she sighed, "but Gary's totally winding me up today; there are times when I really, truly want to lamp him one."

"So do we all," laughed Brian. "Join the club; we've got tee-shirts." But then it seemed to occur to him that maybe a little more was required on this particular occasion. "Want me to go and get you a cup of tea?" he asked.

Greta shrugged. "No thanks, that's okay; you've got to sort out about the tickets anyway, haven't you?" And, by the looks of things, the sooner Brian got himself into the line of people shuffling through the Portakabin the better it would be for all of them.

"Well, all right. If you're quite sure you're okay."

"I'll be fine," she said. "I'll stay here with Gus; at least he's tall enough to keep the wind off me." And she made an elaborate pantomime of tucking herself into the shelter Angus offered, and watching Brian's progress as he strode off confidently across the car park.

Dennis had been watching all this with faint amusement, although he couldn't put his finger on why he found it quite so entertaining, and now he turned away from the wind to light a cigarette – only to discover Allan standing quietly at his side.

"Oh, hello," he said, and heard with amazement the slight fondness in the tone of his own voice. "Smoke?"

"Thanks." Allan took one and permitted Dennis to light it for him. "Well," he said, "we'll soon be home."

"Yes, I suppose so. I reckon this trip will have changed one or two things, though. Not just for us, I mean."

"Yeah, you're right." Unnecessarily, Allan doffed his ash. "Those two, for a start."

"Eh? Which two d'you mean?"

"Gary and Greta. She's had just about enough of him, Dennis, can't you see that? She was always too good for him anyway, that much was obvious; I reckon she deserves better than a wanker who reads second-hand porn and collects coloured toilet seats. Not to mention that he's homophobic into the bargain," he added, as though that was the clinching argument.

"What, because of the things he said about Mick Jagger? That's not homophobia that's ... well, he's just a bit on the thick side, that's all."

"That's easy enough to say," countered Allan, "but would you really want him knowing anything about last night? Don't you think it would be all round the hospital in five minutes flat if he did, and the pair of us would be looking through the 'Situations Vacant' pages five minutes after that?"

"Well, now that you put it that way," Dennis acknowledged, "maybe not. I don't think he's homophobic in particular, though; I think he's just everything-phobic. Foreigners, Arsenal fans ... and probably women as well."

"Which only goes to prove that Greta would be better off with somebody else," was the rational response. "Just about anybody else, in fact. I'd hate to see her tied up for life to a bollock-brain like Gary, wouldn't you?"

"True. I can't really imagine anyone ever wanting to be married to him in the first place, actually. But anyway, Greta could do with somebody a bit more sensible and not quite so bloody loud."

"Exactly. Somebody a bit more like Brian, perhaps? Had you ever thought of that?"

"Brian?" Dennis repeated the name in puzzlement. "You reckon that's a possibility, do you?"

Allan shrugged. "Your guess is as good as mine," he admitted, ruefully, "but I've had a bit of time to think about things this morning while you were driving, and something struck me about Greta that I hadn't actually realised before."

"Oh?" Allan was rationing his words out like drops of blood, and it was incredibly fucking cold out here on the side of the approach road, which was also rather trying to Dennis's patience. They had found a low metal barrier beyond which was a view out towards the grey rolling sea, and they were leaning on it, side by side as though draped nonchalantly over the rail of an ocean liner. There, however, the resemblance ended. "What about her?"

"Not her, exactly. 'Greta', as a name, I mean. Did you know it was a short form of 'Margaret'."

"No, I never knew that. But what exactly has that got to do with the price of chips, anyway?"

"Not a lot," Allan answered, smiling. "Although it could have something to do with why our Greta ended up with a migraine." Then, in the face of Dennis's increasing annoyance, he carried on robustly. "'Greta' and 'Marguerite' are basically the same name," he said. "You, me, Gary, Dennis and Gus, we all had our equivalents, didn't we, in the past? So why shouldn't Greta have had one, too? And why shouldn't her equivalent still be alive?"

"Why not? Because ... well, because ... " And there Dennis stopped. There should have been a good reason, of course, and he should have known what it was, but somehow he couldn't wrap his brain around it just at the moment. "All the others were dead," was what he said eventually, although he was aware of the weakness of the argument.

"Okay, I'm prepared to accept that. But all it does is rule out ghosts and reincarnations," answered Allan. "If I'm right, and it was something to do with the place itself ... "

" … then all bets are off, yeah, I understand that. So if your man or mine had happened to still be alive we could easily have run into them, couldn't we?"

"Well, yes … except that I think it was their being dead that made it all so bloody necessary in the first place. They wanted us to finish what they started, didn't they? That was what last night was all about, after all."

"Oh, yeah, right. So you're telling me we're not the only ones with unfinished business? What you're saying, in effect, is … "

" … that maybe Marguerite and her Honourable Bryant are also going to get another chance? Yes, that's precisely what I'm saying, Dennis. In fact I'll have a fiver on it with you; I bet Greta and Brian will be an item by this time next year."

"A fiver." Dennis reached out and offered to shake him by the hand. "All right, mate, you're on."

Allan's fingers slid easily into his and they shook briefly, but it was not quite so straightforward to let go afterwards as it should have been. There was still some form of residual current that arced between them, just the very slightest static tingle to remind them of everything that had passed.

"And how about us?" he continued, gruffly. "Is that all over now, or do you reckon there's any future in it?"

"I don't know – and I'm surprised you even asked the question. I'm not exactly any kind of a bargain, Dennis; my ex-wife ended up hating me, and for all I know you probably will too. Plus I don't … I mean, I've never actually had a proper relationship with a bloke before and I wouldn't really know where to start – and to be quite honest I wouldn't have thought it was anything you'd be interested in, yourself."

"Which is more or less the point, I suppose." Dennis shifted awkwardly, from one foot to the other. "I haven't got a bloody clue about this sort of stuff either, but I'd be perfectly willing to give it a try – assuming you wanted to, that is. As long as we could keep it off everybody else's radar, anyway, at least to start with."

"And by 'anybody else', presumably you mean Gary?"

"By 'anybody else' I mean Gary, yes. But, you know, last night … well … "

"Yes. It was pretty good, wasn't it?"

"It was," admitted Dennis, with a smile. "It was bloody good, in fact. So anyway, now that we seem to have got the hang of that sort of thing all right, and I reckon that really should have been the difficult bit – well, there's a good chance we'll get a grip on the rest of it at some stage. If we're willing to work at it, like."

"The rest of it?" There was quiet amusement in Allan's tone.

"You know what I mean. The kind of stuff that isn't sex. The kind of stuff people do when they're … courting, if you want."

"Courting. Now there's a nice old-fashioned word for it! Oh, it's all right, Dennis, I'm not taking the piss out of you. In fact I think you've got a very good point; sex is the easy part, but actually working on the friendship … well, that takes longer. No unrealistic expectations, though; I like the idea of that."

"Good. Well, then, how about we get together some time and watch *Ghostbusters*, for a start? I've got it on video at home," he added, grinning. "Maybe one of the weekends when Angus goes up to Scotland to see his mum? Then you could stay over at my place – that is, if you wanted to."

"All right. That sounds very much like a plan."

"It does, doesn't it? Well, it's as close to one as we're likely to get, anyway." If the exchange of sheepish grins was anything to go by, this was a determination which seemed to suit them both. "And how about football? We could go to another game together some time, couldn't we?"

"We could," Allan told him cautiously. "If you and Gus are thinking of running a trip to Sweden in June for the group stages, for example, I'd probably be on for that. You can get a car ferry from Newcastle to Denmark, and drive into Sweden from there."

"Well, I'm not sure." This was a completely new idea to Dennis, one that had not even remotely crossed his radar before, but now that he thought about it there were certainly attractions to the concept. "If Gus thinks the van'll be up to it," he said, thoughtfully, "I wouldn't be entirely opposed."

"Well, then, potentially – perhaps the two of us could share a room again?"

"I wouldn't rule it out," conceded Dennis, grinning. "Not before that, though? You wouldn't want to go to any domestic fixtures with me?"

Allan's expression darkened. "Well, possibly not," he conceded, ruefully. "I'm not sure our interests are entirely compatible, you see, what with you being a Newcastle fan. Your team and mine are deadly rivals, I'm afraid."

"Oh? And what's that supposed to mean, then, when it's out walking? Wait a minute, you're not trying to tell me you're a bloody 'monkey hanger' after all, are you? I thought that was all just something I made up on the spur of the moment, like."

"No, I'm not a 'monkey hanger', but I have a nasty idea you'll probably wish I was. It's even worse than that, I'm sorry to say; in fact, I'm actually a 'smoggie'."

"A 'smoggie'? What, you follow bloody Middlesbrough, do you mean?"

"I'm afraid so – although I'm not really apologising for it, you understand. There wasn't actually a lot I could do about it, living in Catterick all that time."

"Well, it's a bit of a scunner is that," Dennis told him gravely. "But at least you're willing to admit it, which I believe is the first step towards finding a cure. There is hope, you know, or so I've heard, but it'll probably take while."

"So we won't be going to any football matches in the immediate future, then?" asked Allan, with a smile.

"No, we won't," came the firm response. "Not until you're feeling better, anyway."

"That's a bit of a shame, really, isn't it?"

"Well, it is, but never mind – there's plenty of other stuff a pair of blokes like us can do together in their spare time that we wouldn't have to fall out over. Apart from the obvious, I mean. What about cricket, do you like that at all? Only we could maybe go to something in the summer? There's the Scarborough Festival, for example," Dennis concluded, sudden misgivings threatening to undermine his confidence.

Happily, Allan sighed. "Well, thank goodness for that," he said. "I was beginning to think we were going to have a problem there for a minute! Yes, as a matter of fact, I do like cricket – very much. And we've got a World XI playing Pakistan at Scarborough some time in August, haven't we? I quite fancy seeing that, I must admit."

"Yes," said Dennis, "me too. So we'll go to that together then, shall we?"

"I think I'd like to, definitely," was the cautious response. "If it's all still going on by that stage, I mean."

Which, thought Dennis to himself, was precisely the point. They could make just as many tentative jam-tomorrow, pie-in-the-sky plans as they liked, but whether or not their relationship would survive in the future as well as it had in the distant past was another matter entirely.

"All right, then," he said, cautiously, "it's a deal. You know, Allan, I've got a strange idea that this just might be the start of a beautiful friendship."

And Allan, at his side, sniggered in response to this – as a result of which, Dennis really didn't doubt it any more.

Despite Brian's breezy assurance that it would only be a question of showing up, presenting their Turdo tickets and their confirmation number, and paying the nominal fare, the formalities in the Portakabin seemed to take longer than expected. In the end they were all so cold and so tired of waiting that Gus unlocked the van again and everyone got back in except Gary who, having consumed his cup of tea in record time, was now determined to dispose of it again just as rapidly. When he came loping back across the forecourt, though, it was with a less than impressed expression on his face.

"White," he said. "Bloody boring. We'll just have to cash in all our bets, then, I suppose; not likely to encounter too many rainbow-coloured plumbing fixtures on the other side of the Channel, are we?"

"Well, why don't we just have one last round on the boat?" suggested Dennis, feeling brighter and more optimistic than he had in quite some time, and fully prepared to share the improvement in his temper with the rest of the world if he had to – even if the rest of the world only consisted of Gary.

"All right, then." He hadn't taken a great deal of persuading, after all.

Not long after that, however, the door of the Portakabin swung open and Brian made a beeline for the minibus, waving a bunch of papers in his hand like Neville Chamberlain arriving home after the Munich peace-talks.

"Got them!" he yelled. "We can go on board the ferry now."

"Thank fuck for that," responded Dennis, strapping on his seat-belt and turning the key in the ignition even before Brian had made it back as far as the vehicle. "You're a bloody genius with this stuff, Brian."

"Oh aye," added Gus, as Brian clambered into his seat. "Brian's definitely your man when it comes to sorting out ferries and suchlike."

"Well, he would be, wouldn't he?" asked Gary, brightly. "He's Brian bloody Ferry, isn't he?"

"Brian Ferry? Oh my God, that's awful! That is officially the worst pun in the history of the world ever."

"Oh no it isn't!" yelped Gary, and launched into a selection of others of equal lack of merit just to prove it.

Brian, however, seemed to take it all in good part, presumably reasoning – as Dennis had, and no doubt most of the others, too – that any nickname Gary chose to bestow would have been forgotten about or replaced by another within the week. This one wasn't such a bad one as all that, either, and maybe it even stood a chance of lasting. They had better think about recruiting Brian to help them organise the Sweden trip, then; that way they might stand a reasonable chance of getting home again by the same route they had gone out.

Brian had turned in his seat now and was looking across towards Dennis, with an expression of long-suffering pain etched into his features.

"Come on, then, Den," he said, "let's go. We've still got a long way to go on the other side, so let's get up this bloody ramp and into this bloody ship before anything else has a chance to go wrong; I just can't wait to get back home."

Which was a sentiment with which Dennis was only too willing to concur, and therefore without further ado he let out the handbrake, let in the clutch, rolled the minibus forward, and resolutely turned its nose towards England.

About Adam Fitzroy

Imaginist and purveyor of tall tales Adam Fitzroy is a UK resident who has been successfully spinning male-male romances either part-time or full-time since the 1980s, and has a particular interest in examining the conflicting demands of love and duty.

Made in the USA
Charleston, SC
07 April 2015